LATTES AND
LULLABYES

Seaside Sisters Series

KAY LYONS

Kindred Spirits Publishing

Chapter 1

"Hello there, young lady. It's good to see you," a man said as he crossed over the threshold into London's Lattes.

London Cohen smiled and greeted the older gentleman. "Hey, Dally! Where have you been hiding yourself?"

"Oh, you know how it is. Staying busy. Thought I'd come gaze at your pretty mug before going to see what's biting at the pier."

"Aww, I'm glad you stopped in. You want your usual?"

The older man nodded his gray head and London tried as she always did to pinpoint his age. She'd guess him to be in his sixties, though to look at him, seventy wouldn't be a stretch. Still, she couldn't help but think the deep lines and wrinkles were more from a life hard lived than the Carolina sun.

"It amazes me how you remember. Haven't been able to make it in for a while."

"Ah, but trying to remember my customers' orders helps keep me sharp," she said, tapping a finger to her temple before setting to work on his large decaf coffee with half-and-half and two sugars.

"Saw on the internet where you were honored for serving food and coffee to the emergency aid workers after the storm."

She'd never get used to people calling a hurricane a simple "storm," but she supposed as a coastal native, Dally had earned his salt-life credentials. "I was happy to do it. It was a nice evening."

Last September, the monster Cat 5 hurricane had been downgraded to a Cat 1 before hitting the Wilmington, North Carolina, area, but it had still caused extensive damage to homes and businesses. Roofs were blown off, trees downed, roads blocked, flooding. But farther inland, the damage had been far worse with record-setting floods due to the rain that just kept coming.

The moment she'd been able to open her doors, she'd brewed as much coffee as the power crews, emergency services, police, and recovery volunteers could drink. Post-hurricane clean-up was a community event that included coffee and encouragement. The recognition BBQ had been nice, but nine months after last year's hurricane meant watching the spaghetti models and Atlantic again, the other definition of salt-life living.

A shadow formed on the other side of her door just as she set Dally's cup of brew in front of him, and she cocked her head to get a better glimpse of her next customer. Instead of growing in size, however, the shadow shrank as a golden retriever appeared.

The large dog hesitated on the threshold before entering with a familiar tongue-hanging tilt of his beautiful head as he stared at them. "*Rocco?* Is that *you?*"

Dally swiveled on the barstool to face the door.

The golden's entire body wriggled with every tail wag as London quickly made her way around the counter, meeting Rocco halfway, where he'd stopped to survey the nearly empty coffee shop and her dachshund Rosie's empty bed. "Oh, Rocco, it *is* you," she said after a quick glance at his collar. "Hey, buddy. Where have you been? I've missed you."

London knelt on her cleaned and polished floor and lavished the animal with rubs and pets and even a few kisses, all the while hoping that maybe this time she could meet Rocco's owner. Whoever owned the precious dog had to know what a joy the well-behaved canine was.

Rocco had appeared out of the blue in May, alone and seemingly worn out. He'd visited a few times for a period of about a week, but even though both London and her sister Ireland had called the number on Rocco's collar, the owner hadn't returned the calls. Rocco appeared, curled up beside Rosie, and slept, then got up and left once nap time was over, enjoying a few head pats and *good boy* praises on his way out the door.

Then, Rocco had simply stopped visiting. "Don't worry. Your girlfriend is—" Rosie's collar bell jingled as the little dog made her way out of her den behind the counter and quickly ran to greet their visitor. "See? She's missed you, too."

"Don't forget me," Dally said from behind them, drawing Rocco's attention. "C'mere, boy."

The dog hurried over to Dally and rubbed himself against the man's legs. Dally lavished the dog with attention, looking a bit misty-eyed for a moment.

"Hey, there, Rocco. How you doing, buddy?"

"Dally," London said, frowning at the man's thickened voice. "You okay?"

"Ah, fine. Just fine. Today's been full of good news is all."

"Oh? Wanna share? I could always use some good news."

Dally smiled down in Rocco's sweet face. "Well, Rocco's back… and my son's in town."

"That's wonderful! So you've talked? Things between you are okay now?"

Baristas and bartenders had a few things in common, one being that people had a tendency to pull up a stool and talk when things were slow. Or the customers felt low.

Dally was one of those people. He'd stopped in for coffee one day and lingered, sharing just enough information for London to know all was not right with his world when it came to his family.

"No, no. Nothing as good as that. But I like knowing Scout's close by, even if I don't get to talk to him."

"Hey, you never know. Maybe it's the first step and you'll reconnect soon."

Rocco and Rosie greeted each other, but then the larger dog looked around the interior of the nearly empty business before giving her a slow, brown-eyed blink. "Don't gimme that look," she stated defensively. "You haven't been here to look all cute with Rosie for everyone to post on social media. Rocco and Rosie were quite the attraction," she said to Dally, shoving herself to her feet and returning to the counter where Dally sat. "You wouldn't believe how many people have stopped in hoping to see the two of them together because they'd seen them online. They were four-legged celebrities."

"They are a pretty sight."

Dally sipped his coffee and he and London both watched the dogs as Rocco followed Rosie to the dog bed across the room.

"Hmm, maybe this time I *shouldn't* call your owner so you'll be able to come back."

"Uh-oh. Better make a run for it while you can, Dally," London's sister Frankie said as she entered the coffee shop.

"Especially if London's talking about locking up customers to keep them here."

The older man chuckled and shook his head at them. "You girls make me laugh every time I come in here."

"Tough job, but we try. How have you been, Dally?"

London listened to the exchange between the two while taking in Frankie's military-issue shorts and camouflage tank top. How could anyone could wear such an ugly color of green and still look feminine? Somehow Frankie pulled it off though. Her twin was the most rough-and-tumble of them all, but London knew her sister hid a soft side beneath the tough shell. The scars Frankie carried visibly were nothing compared to the pain and damage they represented.

"I'm good. Can't look at those two and not feel good." The man pointed a finger toward the animals.

Frankie moved deeper into the interior. "They are pretty cute together. Rocco's people must be visiting again."

London crossed her arms over her front and sighed. "I really don't want to call again, but I guess I have to, don't I?"

"Maybe not. If the timing is right, I can follow him home and see where he lives," Frankie said.

"That's a good idea. I am *really* curious. You want some coffee?"

"Oh, yeah. Strong and black."

"This late in the afternoon? You know my thoughts on that."

Frankie leaned against the counter beside Dally, nudging the older man with an elbow. "Londy here believes only uptight, type-A personalities drink black coffee."

"Is that true?" Dally asked, amusement lighting his tired, darkly shadowed eyes.

Frankie grinned and winked at the man.

"You got a big project you're working on?" Dally asked.

"Several, but not today. Just playing catch-up. I need to put in some hours at the shop and make sure the monkeys didn't get too crazy while I was away. Today was my volunteer day."

The reminder explained Frankie's freshly washed and still damp hair. Frankie was hands on and didn't mind getting dirty, so she'd often wound up far from the hurricane relief setups handing out bottled water or helping with paperwork, instead jumping in the trenches mucking out water-logged homes. With so much damage, homes were still being repaired as a new hurricane season kicked into gear. "What was it today? More demo?"

Frankie shrugged like it was no big deal that she voluntarily donned protective clothing and breathing masks to go in and clean out dangerous mold for total strangers.

"Yeah. The vultures are *really* circling, trying to buy up houses for nothing because of the damage and the financial strain families are feeling having to pay a mortgage on a house they can't live in while trying to pay rent somewhere else to keep a roof over their heads *and* deal with insurance companies, some of which are really shady. It amazes me how disaster brings out the best in some but the worst in others."

London paused long enough to shoot Frankie a look of pride and genuine love. Her sister had followed in their father's footsteps and enlisted at eighteen, served her country for ten years, then got out a year ago after being injured when the convoy she was traveling in struck an IED. Though the scars weren't visible unless Frankie donned a two-piece, the damage had been severe, though mostly internal. Once she'd recovered, Frankie had settled in Carolina Cove in time to assist with hurricane recovery and put her mechanics training and experience to use by buying out a tow and repair shop that hired vets like her.

"What?" Frankie looked from London to Dally. "Why is she looking at me like that?"

Dally shook his head at her and took another sip before saying, "Girl, you oughta recognize love when you see it."

"What he said," London said simply.

Frankie, the sister most uncomfortable with her emotions, rolled her eyes.

"Yeah, whatever."

"Hey, face it. You're a pretty cool person to have as a twin. I appreciate the fact you've never been boring. That's all."

"O-kay." Frankie raised a dark and well-groomed eyebrow.

Of the five sisters, Frankie's hair was the darkest, a deep, chocolate brown that made her blue eyes stand out even more. London's hair was a lighter brown, while Carolina's, Holland's, and Ireland's ranged from sandy, brownish-blond to auburn.

"So what about you?" Frankie asked Dally. "You feeling okay today?"

"I'm good."

London busied herself with fetching Frankie's coffee.

"You sure? You're looking a little pale considering all of that sun out there."

"Ah, I'm fine, hon. Just some old issues catching up with me."

"Well, if there's anything we can do to help, say the word."

"Absolutely," London said, handing over the oversized

cup. "You're part of our family now and don't you forget it."

Dally frowned and became misty-eyed once more.

"Ah, you girls. You don't know what that means to me. I hope one day my son finds a sweet girl like one of you."

Frankie winked at London and straightened on the stool, a teasing, ornery expression falling into place.

"Oh, yeah? Which one?"

Chapter 2

Cooper Bale stared at the blinking cursor with gritty eyes. One of the twins let loose an ear-splitting scream in the living room, and the sound shredded his nerve endings. His almost-four-year-old niece and nephew were in rare form today after a restless night, which had left their recently hired nanny, Michelle, juggling the twins like a circus performer.

He leaned back in his office chair and pressed his palms to his eyes, attempting to rub the grittiness away. He'd gotten up with the twins last night as well, but short of turning whichever twin he held away from him so they focused on Michelle, he hadn't been much help in the kid-soothing department. He believed when they looked at him they saw him as the man who took them away from their mother and grandmother, even though he knew at their age that kind of thinking was unlikely.

The crying stopped and he listened to the soft tones of Michelle singing to them, trying to get them to join her. He scrubbed his hands over his face and tried to focus again, but the sound of footsteps approaching his office door left him muttering under his breath. A soft knock sounded. "Come in."

"Hey," Michelle said, Bella on her hip. "Sorry to interrupt but I needed to separate them and… I thought you might be able to use this." She carried a large steaming mug toward him and set it on his desk by his arm.

"Thanks."

"My pleasure." Releasing the cup, she moved her hand to his wrist and gently squeezed. "I know your deadline is looming, but you can do this. No worries."

Cooper stared at the polished fingers lingering on his wrist and sucked in a breath. Uh… surely he was misreading things? He was eleven years her senior and her boss. But Michelle had been finding excuses to touch him more and more, brushing against him as she walked by, grasping his hand or arm as she spoke to him or transferred one of the twins to him to carry. She couldn't think there was a chance he'd—

His cell phone buzzed and he used the opportunity to extract himself. No doubt it was his client requesting an update. Again. As he shifted away from her in the office chair, his hand settled on the device and he swiped to answer without looking at the number. "Bale."

"Um, hello? Is this Rocco's family?"

"Yes. Yes, hang on a second, please." To Michelle, he said, "I have to take this. Shut the door on your way out?"

The beautiful nanny pinned a smile to her lips and shook her head.

"Of course. Let me know when you need a refill."

Michelle carried his niece out of the office, but there was no way to mistake the look she gave him as she locked gazes before slowly shutting the door behind them.

Cooper closed his eyes and sat back in his office chair. First the twins acting out, Michelle being…*friendly*, and now his dog? At this rate he'd never meet his deadline. "Sorry. I'm here. Rocco's escaped again?"

"I'm afraid so. He hasn't been a bother, but he's here, at London's Lattes on Third, and I, uh, close in about an hour."

"I'll come get him."

"Thank you. And just so you know, I don't mind his visits. Truly. He's such a good dog. He's been here before. I, um, called then, too?"

He closed his eyes with a grimace. That trip. His mother had wanted to see the ocean one last time before she passed, see where the twins would be living, growing up... Just before they were to leave Charlotte to travel to Carolina Cove, his girlfriend had given him the ultimatum of choosing between her and the life they'd planned—or adopting the twins because they had no one else capable of giving them the life a child deserves. A compromise didn't seem to be possible, so she'd walked—run—away as fast as she could. "Yeah. Sorry about not getting back with you. I was here for... Well, things were a little hectic."

"Oh, no problem. I just worry about Rocco being picked up by Animal Control or hit by a car making his way home."

"Yeah, me, too. I'm not sure how he's getting out of the yard, but I'll take another look at the fence. Give me ten minutes to come get him."

In the background, one of the twins took the crying to a whole other level. Bedtime could not come soon enough, and no doubt Michelle could use a little privacy and quiet time herself. Maybe *that* was why she kept seeking him out? Was it her way of asking for help? For him to step up more than he had? But that was why he'd hired her. To take care of them so he could work and keep a roof over their heads.

"Maybe fifteen," he said since there was no disguising the noise in the background. "Did you say coffee shop?"

Michelle had come highly recommended by friends of friends of friends who'd said she worked for an agency overseas for four years before deciding to return to the States. He'd considered himself lucky to snag her on such short notice, especially since she'd already stuck through the hard transitions of his mother dying and girlfriend leaving.

"Yes. London's Lattes." The woman gave him the exact address and Cooper eyed his laptop and then the clock on the wall. "Don't let Rocco leave. I'm only a block away. I'll be there as soon as I can."

Cooper pressed the button to end the call and gathered up his things. The woman said she closed in about an hour, but he could get a lot done in that amount of uninterrupted time.

Backpack ready, he left his office and found Michelle had both kids strapped into their high chairs, eating an assortment of banana slices, yogurt, and cheerios.

"Sorry about all of the noise. Harry grabbed a toy from her and Bella was having none of it."

Harry and Bella. His kid sister had named her children after Harry Potter and Bella from *Twilight*. Examples of the fantasy worlds she'd tried so hard to escape into in order to remove herself from the reality of her own life as an addict and child of an alcoholic.

Cooper nodded, though there wasn't much about the situation he understood. After the childhood he and Ashley had experienced, he'd planned on never having kids, and his current reality wasn't something he'd envisioned, though he felt compelled to do. And poor Rocco—another gift for his girlfriend to keep her company when he had to travel—had been left behind just like he had. "You'll be okay if I head out for a while?"

"We'll be fine." Michelle smiled confidently. "After a snack, dinner, and some playtime in the bath, it'll be bedtime. We're almost there."

Almost was a long way from *there*.

Cooper managed a tired smile at the kids staring at him with their tear-smeared and wary expressions. Almost four or not, he had to believe that to them he was just another man who'd appeared in their life out of nowhere. He also knew they'd learned the hard way to be wary, but he was just as stressed as they were to accept the new norm.

Cooper chose to steer clear of the duo, hoping to spare the nanny more turmoil if their emotions flared once more. "Rocco's escaped again. I'm going to pick him up and… try to get some work done for my deadline."

"I was afraid of that. He went racing out the doggie door when Bella finally left him alone."

"He's adjusting to the move and the changes like the rest of us. Right, guys?" Bella stared at him like he was a monster about to devour her, and she puckered her lip to cry because of it.

"No," the little girl stated firmly.

"You said it," Cooper said, winking at the little girl.

Michelle laughed as though he was a comedian and flashed him another blinding smile, and Cooper lifted his hand in a silent goodbye.

Michelle had his cell if she needed him, but everyone in the room knew who was best at handling the twins. The twenty-two-year-old had the skills and know-how to deal with them, whereas he… wasn't sure what to do. Nothing made the twins happy for long. Short of being a human bouncy or handing them sippy cups, which they promptly threw in their upset, he was at a loss.

The five-minute walk to the coffee shop helped clear his head and eased the knot drawing his shoulders up to his ears. He'd used the sidewalks to get there, having to walk down the street to the main road, down a block, and back south to the address. But as he did so, Cooper realized Rocco probably crossed from their yard into their neighbors' property and headed between the structures to the building housing London's Lattes. As the crow flew—or dog traveled—the coffee shop was only two backyards away and easily accessible.

A low woof greeted Cooper as he entered the coffee shop, but it was the woman behind the counter that drew his immediate attention with her light brown hair and bright green eyes that pierced him from across the room.

"That's the first time I've heard him bark. You must be Rocco's dad? I'm London Cohen."

London. The name suited her. Regal. Unique. It matched the eclectic cuteness of the coffee shop that looked to be a mixture of coffee and sandwiches, ice cream, beach-and-coffee-themed souvenirs, and comfortable gathering spots he eyed with pathetic excitement. "Cooper Bale. Nice to meet you," he said, turning his attention back to her. He closed the distance between them and shook her outstretched hand. "Thanks for watching out for him."

"My pleasure. Like I said, Rocco's never a bother. In fact, I've always been curious as to how old he is?"

"Three."

"Oh."

Her frown deepened at his words, and he followed her gaze to where Rocco lay on the floor beside a little wiener dog.

"I would've guessed him to be older. Rocco comes in, lies down, and sleeps by Rosie like he's completely worn out."

Tired as he was after last night's scream-fest, Cooper sympathized with the dog. "He doesn't get a lot of time to himself at home. The twins rarely leave him be unless he manages to hide somewhere."

"Oooh, no wonder he's such a tired boy. How old are your twins?"

London had moved closer to the animals and now bent to pet Rocco's head. Cooper watched, drawn even deeper into the empty coffee shop because of the dog—and the woman. Still, he was unsettled as always by the mention of "his" twins. "Uhh, going on four. A boy and a girl."

"Oh, that's a lot of energy in little packages. And cool that they're twins. I'm a twin, too."

There were two of her? London Cohen wasn't hard to look at, and any red-blooded male would appreciate the sight of her dressed in white shorts and a simple black T-shirt with London's Lattes in silver script that looked like steam over a coffee mug on the back.

Cooper watched as London's thick braid fell over one shoulder when she shifted her weight to combat Rocco's when he leaned against her legs. The sparkles on her flip-flops caught the light. She wore a ring with a little dangle on the middle red-polished toe of her right foot.

Cooper shifted his gaze back to her face, wondering how a toe ring and sparkling green eyes nearly had his tongue hanging out of his mouth like Rocco's. "Uhh, trust me, Rocco gets more sleep than I do at this point."

"Aww, well, I'm sure it'll get better. Just a phase, right? How about a coffee?" she asked. "Or maybe a protein ball to boost the energy level?"

Rocco lowered himself to the floor, head on his paws,

and closed his eyes. A pretty good indicator that to leave meant carrying the seventy-pound animal out of there if he tried to make the dog leave before Rocco was ready. "Yeah, please. I have some work I need to get done, but I won't keep you past closing. I'll take a coffee, black."

Cooper noted London's gaze narrowed upon hearing his coffee selection.

"Sure thing. Grab a seat. I'll bring it right out."

Chapter 3

Once settled in front of his computer, Cooper went to work with a passion and intensity London found oddly fascinating. Whatever he did for a living, he loved it, and it showed. Too bad he favored plain, black coffee, she mused, smiling to herself. Type A all the way.

Once again, London found her gaze on him before she forced herself to look away in fear of him catching her in the act of ogling him. She couldn't help it though. Ever since the first day of Rocco's appearance, she'd wondered about the dog's owner. Whether Rocco's human was male or female, a family with rambunctious kids. Now she knew. Well, almost. Obviously Rocco's person was male, but whether there was a significant other or a Mrs. Cooper Bale in the picture remained to be seen. The kids though...

Cooper had mentioned children—twins, no less—but short of asking questions she had no right to ask, her curiosity would have to just chill. Though truth be told, she had a hard time believing a man like Cooper *wouldn't* be attached to someone, especially with two little ones running around. That was usually a package deal kind of thing.

Standing a couple of inches over six feet, Cooper's lanky but muscular form was dressed in casual shorts and a navy T-shirt, boat shoes on his feet. Handsome, with whiskey-brown eyes and dark hair that was short on the sides and longer on top, combed back in that style that was popular once more today, he didn't fit her image of a guy who spent his days behind a computer screen.

But there he was, tapping madly away at the keyboard in front of him, though given his lack of Carolina "bronzing," she supposed he was indoors more than out.

She'd seen plenty of men come through her coffee shop with laptops in tow, wanting a quiet place to work. Those in town on business were usually in khakis and polos. Vacationers hunting free Wi-Fi typically sported swim trunks and tees. But the gamers... they inevitably wore an assortment of black shirts and dark shorts or pants, picking the darkest corner of the building to play video games while downing double shots of espresso. It was amazing how people wore—and drank—their personalities, and studying them fascinated her to no end.

Cooper continued to type, and she went to work behind the counter, taking inventory for her next order and doing general upkeep and cleaning.

Opening the coffee shop had been her passion. One she'd pursued with intensity and zeal equal to that Cooper displayed. She'd studied business and coffee, marketing and trends. Anything and everything she might possibly need to know in order to get her business off the ground and make it successful.

And it was. Despite the less-than-stellar location off the main road running through Carolina Cove, despite the lag post-hurricane due to rental cancellations and damage, people still found her. Coffee addiction was a hefty draw, after all, and all the rage from tweens on up. That's why she covered all the bases, with ice cream and candy for the non-coffee customers and gourmet dog treats for the four-legged fur kids.

Closing time came and went, and even though she knew she ought to clear her throat or inform Cooper of the hour, she simply went about prepping for tomorrow morning like she always did. It wasn't like he disturbed her or kept her from doing what needed done. She cleaned tables and removed trash from the bins and worked on her chalkboard for tomorrow's special.

When those things were completed and Cooper *still* typed, she moved behind the counter to catch up on the paperwork she'd put off and neglected for longer than she cared to admit.

She might have bordered type A at one point when getting through school and her business off the ground, but she'd backslid over the years into a mix of A and B. Residing on the coast, on an island, no less, had softened the rushed urge for total control into the more relaxed pace of vacation-destination living. It was all out of her control anyway, so why get that bent out of shape about things? If it was going to happen, it would. Period. More often than not, she had to remind herself of that fact, repeatedly, but on a good day, reminders weren't needed.

She'd just finished the last of the data entry when Cooper muttered something and rose from his table. He met her gaze with an apologetic look and quickly walked toward the counter.

"London, I'm sorry. I only meant to stay until closing, but I got on a roll and… I apologize. I completely lost track of time."

She didn't bother glancing at the clock. "It's fine. No,

really, it is," she said when she saw skepticism flash across his features. "Thanks to you, I managed to get caught up myself." She waved a hand toward the table where he'd sat. "You were hard at it and I didn't want to interrupt. I don't think I've ever seen anyone type that fast."

A deep rumble of laughter left his chest, and he shrugged, looking a little embarrassed and sexy at once. "I've been told I can get pretty intense. You should've seen me when I first started. I was lucky if I had ten characters a minute, but my interest in coding meant picking up speed."

"Coding?"

"I'm a software engineer, and right now I'm behind the eight ball on a program for a pretty big client. I managed to catch up quite a bit in the last couple of hours, though I'm afraid it was at your expense."

"Like I said, it's not a problem. You inspired me to be more productive, and I can now face my accountant fully prepared when the time comes because of it."

He smiled at her words and nodded.

"Glad to hear it. So, uh…"

Silence filled the air and became a bit awkward as they simply gazed at each other. Cooper inhaled before narrowing his gaze.

"Are you hungry? Maybe you would let me officially apologize by taking you to dinner?"

Dinner? "Oh, that's not nec—"

"It's the least I can do after you've watched out for Rocco and stayed two hours past closing because I couldn't dig my head out of my computer."

She tilted her head to the side, liking the way he looked at her but needing to know the answers to some pretty key questions. "Your wife won't mind?"

His expression revealed his amusement. "Since I'm not

married, no, she won't. Do you get asked to dinner by a lot of married men?"

"Can't say it hasn't happened."

"I see. Did you go out with them?"

"No. I told them they needed to go home and date their wives."

His eyes warmed with amusement, and she found herself relaxing in return. The whiskey color of his gaze hypnotized her and made her think of the golden bronze of molten glass.

"Glad to hear it."

"Mmm." Her heart rate picked up speed, and she cocked her head to one side as all sorts of thoughts raced through her mind. "Are you separated? Because being separated doesn't equal divorced. It means married, living separately—which is still married."

He shifted his stance and braced his palms flat against the countertop, his gaze holding hers with an intensity that left her flustered and a little breathless.

"Not married, not separated. Not dating anyone. Single and hungry. For food," he quickly added. "You?"

"I could eat."

A deep, rumbling chuckle emerged from him. "Ah, really? You're going to make me ask? Okay, fine. Are you single, separated, or married?"

"Single and... hungry for food," she said, earning another grin from him when she mimicked his response.

"Good to know. So, have I answered all of your questions?"

"Hardly. My sisters say I'm nosy, but I choose to believe I'm keeping myself informed. It avoids misunderstandings later."

"Sounds perfectly reasonable. How many sisters?"

"Four."

Cooper whistled softly. "I can't imagine five kids. Any brothers?"

"Nope. My poor father, right? Six women under one roof."

His expression shifted to a mixture of awe and horror.

"That is a lot of estrogen. The, uh, kids are my niece and nephew. That's probably why you asked about me being married?"

"I wondered."

"Yeah. I, uh, adopted them. I haven't actually had them for long, so I haven't quite worked out the right way of discussing them."

"I see. Well, you will."

"Mmm."

Cooper's response tweaked her curiosity, but she felt the uncomfortable awareness of a subject too personal to discuss in depth given their three-hour acquaintance. Time would tell if she'd learn more or go on wondering about the specifics. Obviously he wanted to clarify the situation, but why? He wanted the kids or he wouldn't have adopted them. Maybe he felt unworthy of having them? Or, maybe, his type-A mindset simply wanted her to know he wasn't irresponsible.

A quick glance at the table where he'd spent the last several hours working provided backup for her third guess. Not a paper, pen, computer, phone, or paper pad was out of place.

Cooper's stomach growled. Loudly.

"Look, as far as dinner goes, you'd be doing me a huge favor. I wouldn't have to eat alone in a new town, I'd repay your kindness, *and* I'd avoid the chaotic scream-fest that is bedtime."

Unable to resist his charm and wanting to know more about him, she closed the laptop in front of her with a soft thud. Single man with two kids and, no doubt, a story to go with them from what he'd just told her. Dating potential? Debatable. But she admired that he was up-front about it, and she was getting to an age where the odds of meeting someone *without* kids in the mix were fifty-fifty. *Plus, it's a thank-you dinner. No more.* "Where are we going?"

"What's good?"

"Depends on what you're in the mood for." Oh, words to never say to a man, especially a good-looking one. "I mean…"

"Do you like Italian?"

She knew exactly the restaurant he referenced. Eddie's was nice. Small, quiet. Great food. Some might even say it was romantic, depending on the time of year. June was the height of busy season so they'd be too crowded to be considered romantic. "Getting a table without a reservation is a gamble, but let's give it a shot. Carbs *are* pretty awesome, especially after a long day."

She felt an excited flutter in her belly when Cooper held her gaze. She'd always considered brown eyes to be plain and boring, but there in the depths were flecks of bronze-gold and deep mahogany. Nothing plain or boring at all.

"So that's a yes?"

"Yes. I accept your offer because I really don't want to have to figure out what to eat tonight. But I need to lock up and run Rosie upstairs, grab my bag, and freshen up a little…" She plucked at her coffee-splashed T-shirt. Black was a must in a coffee shop.

"How about you do that while I take Rocco home? I'll meet you back here in front of the building in… twenty minutes?"

"That… sounds like a"—*date*—"plan."

Chapter 4

Cooper took Rocco home, made sure the doggie door was firmly locked for the night, and hurried to his room. He raked his fingers through his hair after changing out of the kid-germed shirt he'd worn into a lightweight polo, then quickly brushed his teeth to rid himself of coffee breath, pausing in front of the bathroom mirror. Was he over-dressed? One good thing about moving to a beach town was being able to dress comfortably, especially in the summer heat, and he'd already been here long enough to realize nothing pegged a tourist faster than what they wore.

He stuck with the shirt he'd chosen and smoothed his hair back once more, more nervous than he cared to admit. But having been dumped like a pipe bomb because of the changes in his life and lifestyle, he'd wondered if dating was off the table until the twins turned eighteen. At least this way, London knew he had the twins, so what happened from here… well, happened.

Michelle had the twins in the bathtub, and as he walked to the door to say goodbye, he heard Bella giggling. He peeked inside the room and saw Harry pouring water from cup to cup, while Bella played with a mermaid doll. Maybe the tide had turned and it would be a peaceful night? He certainly hoped so. For all their sakes. "I'm heading out for a bit."

"Again? I put a plate for you in the fridge."

"That's nice of you, thanks. But I'm going out for dinner. I'll be back in a couple of hours."

Did she look disappointed? Upset? Maybe a little ticked?

"You didn't touch the coffee I brought you earlier. Was it too strong?"

"It was fine. The phone call— When Rocco disappears, he's been going to a coffee shop nearby to sleep, so I grabbed some coding time there when I went to pick him up."

"I see."

"Michelle." He checked his watch and winced at the time. He had to go or be late. "Your job is to look after the twins, not wait on me."

"Of course, but I don't mind. I only want to help. I know this has been hard for you."

Deciding to take her words at face value, he nodded. "I appreciate that. It has been. Thanks. But so long as the twins are taken care of, I'm good. Okay?"

"Of course. Bella, Harry, and I will be fine. Pj's and a story, and we're tucked in. I drank some tea, so I thought I'd stay up and watch a movie. Maybe you'll be back in time to join me."

Join her for a movie?

Michelle leaned against the side of the bathtub and smiled up at him. Had she touched up her makeup while he was gone? He supposed to a young twenty-something that was important, but he hoped she hadn't left the twins unattended while doing it.

But after just clarifying her job duties…

It's an offer, that's all. They lived in the same house, shared meals, chores. There was bound to be some awkwardness between them as they adjusted as two adults living together. At least until they settled into a routine. Right? "I don't know when I'll be back, so don't wait up. Thanks, Michelle."

Cooper wasn't sure how to read the nanny's expression in relation to his goodbye, but he left the house and locked them safely inside to begin the walk back to the coffee shop.

Maybe working from home wasn't such a great idea. The proximity, day in and day out. With London's Lattes so close, maybe he'd make it his office for the next week or so. That way he could work toward his deadline in peace and still be near enough to home should Michelle need something in regard to the twins. After that, who knew? Maybe he would make it a habit or look for other places to work remotely.

Yeah, he liked that idea.

Nineteen minutes after walking Rocco home, Cooper stood in front of the coffee shop. He heard a sound behind him and turned to find London leaving the building by a side door. She pulled it closed and double-checked that it locked while he took in her change in appearance.

London had switched from the workday T-shirt to a short-sleeve black top that bared one shoulder. The black sparkly flip-flops remained, but the shorts had been changed for artistically worn and ragged jean shorts that made her legs look even more tan against the faded denim. She'd also added dangly earrings and, if he wasn't mistaken, a touch of perfume and lip gloss. "You look beautiful."

"Thank you. You look nice, too."

They exchanged a long glance before her gaze shifted down to where she tucked her keys into her bag. That done, she joined him on the sidewalk, and Cooper inhaled the alluring scent of her perfume.

"Ready?"

He offered her his arm so that she'd slide that bare shoulder into place next to his as they walked. "How long have you owned the coffee shop?"

"Five years last May."

He narrowed his gaze, trying to figure out her age without having to ask. "You must have been a child when you bought it."

She tilted her head back as she laughed and gave him a sideways glance that said he wasn't nearly as subtle as he would've liked to have been.

"I was twenty-five."

Twenty-five. Which made her thirty now. "I'm thirty-three. In case you're wondering. Any particular reason you focused on coffee?"

"Actually, yeah. It comes from being a military brat," she said, smiling up at him. "No matter where we landed, coffee drew my parents to other people and helped the transition. It didn't matter if it was sharing a cup with a new neighbor or visiting a cafe, I've always liked how coffee bonds people. We may be strangers in the beginning, but having that something in common breaks the ice and gets us talking. And as a bonus, I've gotten pretty good at guessing someone's personality based on their order."

"Sounds like you've got it down to a science."

She nodded firmly. "I try not to brag but I've definitely got a knack for it. You, for example, like order and sched-ules. Am I right?"

He glanced down at her, wondering if she had taken a wild guess or if maybe there was more to her "knack" than he thought. "You are correct. Though right now if you saw my office and house, you'd think a tornado hit it. Between this deadline and the kids' toys and noise, I'm wondering how to make things work. Probably wasn't the smartest idea to move from Charlotte immediately after taking them on, but my one-bedroom apartment there wasn't an option."

"Ah, but how fun to have toys around. You get to be a kid again and see childhood through their eyes in a very different world than when we were kids. If you do software, it's gotta be fun to see them handle electronics we didn't have at that age. Right?"

He pondered her comment in comparison with the way he had been looking at his future with the twins when London waved to someone who then honked the horn. "Friends of yours?"

"Customers, yeah. So, what about you? How *did* you get into software?"

They'd made it to the end of the block but had several to go before reaching the restaurant. Cooper welcomed the change in topic. His childhood wasn't up for discussion. "I wanted a computer. My family didn't have the money to buy one, but the owner of the local computer store said I could take any old parts I needed and build one." Cooper shook his head as he walked, the memories fond though frustrating. "I didn't think I'd ever get that monster to work. But I finally got it going, and from there, nothing could stop me. Coding came next because a computer without software is useless, and the rest is history."

"Wow. I do well to press a button and turn my computer on. I can't imagine building one from scratch. That's amazing."

"Unless you're into it, it's actually pretty boring. But for certain type-A people," he said with a smile, "it's the challenge of taking a blank screen and making it something someone can use. Every program has to be built, so whenever you use an app or even a calculator, it came from a creator."

"I've never thought of it that way. I guess I'm one of those people who've just taken it for granted. Sorry about that."

He shook his head at her apology and laughed softly. "Not a problem. Like I said, it's boring to those it doesn't challenge or who aren't into such things. I'm the odd person who can't get enough. I got a scholarship for college and was hired as soon as I graduated, but I've worked freelance the last five years or so. Mostly for accounting companies, but basically for anyone who needs specialized software. They tell me what they need a computer to do, and it's my job to make it happen."

"That sounds stressful."

"It can be. But so is running your own coffeehouse. Am I right?"

"True," she said, her shiny lips lifting at the corners. "My family thought I was crazy at the time. I mean, I'd worked my way through college as a barista, but when I graduated… I don't know, I think my parents thought I'd go corporate or something. I'll never forget my dad's face when I announced I was buying that building—or that despite my age and freshly inked degree at the time, the bank had agreed to give me a mortgage on it."

"Coffee shop in a beach town. There's a lot of potential if the management is on the ball. I get the impression you are."

London smiled at the praise, and despite the sunglasses covering her eyes, her expression revealed her sense of accomplishment. In that moment, Cooper discovered confidence was a major turn-on for him.

"Thanks. I try to stay on top of things. I can't say it's been easy or everything I've ever dreamed of, but when it comes down to it, I also can't imagine doing anything else as a profession. I like how it helps me get to know my neighbors and community. If you're going to do something every day, you should like it, right? Know that it's your purpose?"

They approached the main road, and the arm he'd given her became a protective hand at her waist as they waited at the crosswalk. Cooper kept an eye out for distracted drivers, and finally traffic paused long enough for them to cross.

Seagulls and grackles made their presence known as they squawked overhead, and in the distance, Cooper spotted a couple of pelicans flying toward the pier. "What was it like growing up with four sisters—and a twin?"

He couldn't help but mirror the grin that crossed her face, even though he wasn't sure why. That was something else he'd noticed about London Cohen and liked. She didn't seem to hold much back. Those smiles of hers were like looking at a sunrise, all bright and engaging, and she wore her thoughts in the many and varied expressions that flickered across her beautiful face.

"It was an adventure to say the least. I always felt sorry for the kids who didn't have siblings. I can't imagine being a military brat and doing everything alone, you know? Everyone knew not to mess with one of us because you got the whole Cohen crew if you did."

He smiled at the image of five combative little girls taking on the playground bully, but it suited her so well. Her background and upbringing were the polar opposite of his, and it piqued his interest in the extreme. What would it have been like to grow up as she had? With seemingly happy, loving parents? Traveling, learning new cultures? Part of a supportive family rather than one generationally dysfunctional?

He was determined to break that curse. That cycle. Provide a life like London's for Ashley's twins and somehow make up for their rough start as children of an addict. It was the least he could do as their uncle. The kids deserved a life of laughter and good memories. But how was he supposed to go about creating something he'd never experienced? Short of hiring competent help capable of caring for them and providing life basics like food and shelter, he didn't feel capable of offering more.

They made it to the restaurant, and Cooper held the door for her, aware they drew the interest of nearly everyone inside, some of whom greeted London with warm familiarity. "Everyone knows you," he said in a low whisper only she could hear.

"Everyone loves coffee," she said, waving at an older couple across the room seated at the bar.

Thanks to a last-minute cancellation, they snagged a quiet corner booth with a red-and-white-checkered tablecloth. Cooper stared at London from across the table, and every shake of her head, every amazing smile, the sway of those earrings back and forth atop her shoulders drew his attention and lured him like a siren calling to sailors at sea.

With every word and flirtatious glance, every belly laugh as she talked about her sisters' antics, he wanted to know more.

And even though he'd just met her, he wanted to touch that bare shoulder. Know if her skin felt as soft as it looked. Get another, closer, deeper whiff of the intriguing scent imprinted in his senses as hers and find out all there was to know about London and her life.

The heaviness of the thought sobered him and brought a surge of unease.

A waitress quickly took their order, and once she walked away, there was a long moment of awkwardness. Cooper found himself blatantly staring at London, unable to look away. Drawn by her on a level he couldn't understand. She was attractive, sure. But this was… different.

"Is something wrong?"

He leaned forward and resettled himself in the seat, leaning on his elbows as he regarded her. "No. Just lost in thought."

"Ah. Still thinking about work?"

He stared into her sea-green eyes and found himself taking the out with an agreeable nod since the mental debate forever going on inside of him wasn't fun and flirtatious dinner conversation. No woman wanted to hear about another woman running away from him as fast as she could. The difficulties the twins could face. The years ahead that could bring disaster after disaster if the cycle repeated itself.

No, tonight he wanted to focus on the fact that London Cohen preferred silver over gold and wore multiple bracelets that jingled every time she lifted her hand to brush an errant curl from her face that the overhead AC kept disturbing. He wanted to enjoy the sweet curve of her lips and the way her eyes lit up when she smiled.

Tonight, he wanted to enjoy dinner with a beautiful woman. Just like he had BK—before kids—when his life had belonged to him.

Chapter 5

London held her glass with both hands and stared across the table at Cooper. She didn't remember ever having a first date as nice as this one. Then again, the fact that this wasn't a date might have something to do with how relaxed she felt talking with him.

Other than the slight awkwardness when she asked about his niece and nephew, they'd chatted nonstop about everything from how she'd started her coffeehouse to her telling him some unique thing about each of her sisters. "Okay, enough about me," she said over her dessert. "How did you and Rocco meet?"

Cooper's rich chuckle warmed the air and caught the attention of the women sitting at the bar. With his dark good looks and that slow, southern drawl of his, she easily understood the appeal and felt the same intrigue. She liked what little she knew of Cooper, but she still couldn't quite peg him. He seemed… reserved, but she wasn't sure if it was his true personality or if something else held him back.

"He found me. I was cutting through an alley in Boston, trying to make a meeting on time after getting waylaid by a delayed flight and a new taxi driver, when I tripped over a garbage bag."

She gasped. "Oh… Don't tell me…"

"Yeah. I'm guessing he'd crawled in after some food, but he had no mama in sight and it was five degrees, if that. I *had* to make that meeting, but I couldn't leave him behind. So, I picked him up and carried him in with me."

"Please tell me the company had a sense of humor about you showing up with a smelly puppy in tow?"

Cooper grinned and the smile warmed his brown eyes to a deep molasses color.

"Rocco got me the contract. The meeting was with the accounting department of a pet supply company, and it just so happened that one of the guys from the meeting was on a smoke break and saw me."

"Yay," she said, smiling as she leaned back in her seat and clapped softly. "I love a happy ending."

"Yeah, me, too. Had I not brought Rocco with me, I'm certain I wouldn't have been hired," he said. "How did you and Rosie meet?"

"*Wellll,* my story isn't as dramatic as yours. I'd done my research and knew I wanted a small dog. My sister—Frankie—thought I was nuts, but she volunteered to help me look. She took me to the rescue center on puppy day and, of all the puppies available, Rosie and I just seemed to hit it off. And get this, Frankie was so taken by the dogs, she contacted the military to adopt one of their retired dogs. He's a German shepherd named Tank."

Cooper laughed at the shepherd's name like almost everyone did and shook his head.

"It's amazing how quickly they get under our skin."

"You've got that right. The first night I brought Rosie home, she wouldn't stop crying, so I wound up letting her sleep in my bed. You know, the whole *it's only for tonight, this isn't going to be a regular thing* lecture pet parents give? Well, she's been there every night since."

Cooper chuckled as he leaned back in the booth, looking relaxed and handsome. The soft white of his shirt contrasted with the warmth of his eyes, and she found herself getting distracted and unable to focus.

"At least she's small. I had to make Rocco sleep on his bed at about six months. He's a kicker. He complains about it every night, too. He has this thing he does that's a combination of whining and backtalk when it's lights out and he has to go to the floor."

She laughed at the image while at the same time fighting the urge to fan her hot face after visualizing Cooper and Rocco snuggled up in tangled sheets. There was just something about a man who cared for and loved his pet, and it was obvious Cooper and Rocco shared a bond. Earlier, after snoozing with Rosie for a while, Rocco had joined Cooper at his table, lying at his human's feet as though he couldn't stand being apart for long.

"They're, uh, starting to clean up."

Cooper's comment pulled her out of her musings, and she glanced across the restaurant to realize they were the only customers remaining. It was obviously closing time, but those familiar to her on the waitstaff were eyeing them —and grinning. Oh, without a doubt, her dinner with Cooper would make the gossip rounds amongst the locals.

"It's a full moon. Would you like to take a walk out on the pier and get a look?"

"Uh…" Was Carolina working the at the pier house tonight? "Sure." Carolina worked every hour she could get between the pier house, Carolina Cove Inn, and the coffee shop, not to mention whatever odd jobs she was able to pick up during the busy season. Her sister saved every penny and used it for her travel fund.

Cooper paid for their meal and, she noted, left a generous tip. Yet another thing that said a lot about a person. There were way too many people in the world who left little to no tip out of sheer greediness, despite the fact service workers depended on them for a large portion of their income and worked hard to earn them. A tip didn't need to be extravagant, just a standard show of kindness and courtesy, and she appreciated that Cooper seemingly felt the same way since he'd also tipped her when he'd paid for his coffees earlier.

Outside, the sun had set, but the area by the pavilion and pier remained well lit and well populated.

It wasn't far to the pier house, and when they walked inside, London breathed a sigh of relief. Carolina wasn't there or else wasn't in sight, and she avoided making eye contact with her father's employees behind the counter.

She and Cooper had separated due to him holding the door for others to enter behind her, and she took advantage and hurried through the building to the rear door leading to the pier. She'd taken several steps up the incline toward the T before Cooper caught up with her.

"In a hurry?"

She laughed and then winced at the awkward sound. "No. Sorry. It's just… I was trying to avoid someone."

Cooper glanced back at the pier house before shifting his attention to her, a thick eyebrow raised high.

"Jealous ex-boyfriend?"

"Worse. Nosy sister. Ireland doesn't usually work nights anymore unless there's an emergency, but Carolina swings between here and the inn. If she sees us, she'll make it a thing and—"

"Wait, Carolina, Ireland, and London?"

She rolled her eyes and wondered if her parents had *any* clue what they'd done by naming their children as they had since it nearly always required an explanation. "Military dad, remember? We were named after where we were conceived."

He narrowed his gaze. "Frankie is for…?"

"France."

"But you're…London," he said, his eyes narrowing in an adorable way.

She wrinkled her nose and laughed. "Yeah, well, let's just say Dad had leave… They weren't quite sure where conception took place, and when there were two of us… Yeah," she added, laughing with him because the story always caused some amusement.

"And your other sister's name is?"

"Holland."

He whistled softly. "Your parents got around."

She giggled as she backed up and turned to lead the way to the T. "That they did."

"Good life, though? Seems like it from the way you've described it."

"Yeah. I mean, it was hard to settle in sometimes only to move again and start a new school when he was reassigned, but it was a great opportunity to meet new people. I have friends all over the world from relationships I made as a kid. The internet has allowed us to keep in touch and stay current."

They slowly walked to the end of the long pier, pausing every now and again to stare at the waves below or the pelicans hanging out, hoping to catch a snack from one of the many fishermen lining the sides.

"Lots of poles in the water tonight."

"Just wait until October. It's shoulder to shoulder with all of the tournaments."

"I've never been here in the off-season."

She looked around them and lowered her voice to a

conspirator's whisper, "Don't tell anyone, but the off-season is the *best* time to be here. No crowds, no long lines, less traffic and noise. It's our own little paradise."

"I can't wait."

They took a few steps in silence before she glanced at him and tried to pry a bit more information out of him. "So… how did you wind up in Carolina Cove? Do you have family here?"

Cooper inhaled and she caught a flash of an expression on his face that she couldn't quite discern.

"No. Growing up, my mom's cousin owned a house here, and every now and again she'd call my mom up and offer it for a week if she wanted to get away. Those were the best summers we ever had. So, when I knew I'd be raising the twins, I had to find something bigger than my one-bedroom in Charlotte, and Carolina Cove came to mind. We visited, which is when you met Rocco the first time, and officially moved in last week."

"Well, I'm glad you did. You'll love it here. It's the quiet months that carry the locals through the crazy ones," she mused with a wry smile. She found an empty bit of railing and leaned against the weather-aged wood to stare out at the waves. The moonlight sparkled atop the water. "Do you surf?"

She sensed she'd probed a little too much if she read his body language correctly, and hoped the change in subject would let Cooper relax again. Some people were more private than others, and she needed to remember that.

In her family, it seemed nothing was confidential, so she had to give allowances to those unused to having every move and decision commented upon.

Cooper leaned against the railing beside her, the act bringing his height down so that his face was closer to hers.

He had the beginnings of crow's feet at the corners of his eyes, but instead of taking away from his looks, she felt they added to them, giving him a cragginess that would only get better with age.

"No. I tried to surf once as a kid. Total disaster."

"Oh, no. Why?"

"I'd found a broken board by the trash and had the bright idea to tape it together. Let's just say it didn't go well."

She laughed at the image his words evoked. "Ah, well, you get a ten for creativity and ingenuity. And now that you're living here, maybe you'll get the chance to try again. There's a surf school where you can get lessons."

"Maybe. We'll see."

She inhaled the warm salt air and looked back toward the shore at the lights shining here and there inside the houses lining the beach. Carolina Cove was family friendly, quiet. Peaceful on a level that was hard to explain to those who'd never visited.

London stifled a yawn and glanced at Cooper to find him watching her.

"Sorry. That was rude." He stared at her with an intensity and directness she found unnerving, but in a good way. A flutter formed deep in her body, born of awareness and mutual interest.

"What time do you get up in the morning?"

She blinked at the question and hated the fact she had to answer honestly. "Mmm. Four thirty," she admitted with a grimace.

He gave her a stern look, his lips forming a slight whistle as he shook his head. "You need to get back and go to bed, huh?"

"Yeah, sorry. I can see myself home if you'd like to stay longer."

He straightened and drew her arm in his, turned them to retrace their steps toward the pier house. "Not a chance. Come on. Let's get you home."

They retraced their steps and talked about some of the gear the fishermen had carted onto the pier. London spotted a couple of well-known local photographers below on the sand, taking shots of the moon over the water. She'd have to remember to look at their social media profiles so she could see the photos.

Inside the pier house, London immediately spotted Carolina helping a customer near the tchotchkes over in the corner. London turned and tried to duck through unnoticed, but Carolina saw them just as Cooper opened the street-facing door. London watched her sister's mouth drop and eyes go wide before London rushed to cross the threshold, praying all the while Carolina wouldn't bolt across the building and outside to demand an introduction.

Walking home didn't take long, especially with them talking the entire way. Cooper asked about her best-selling brew and specifics about the island a newcomer needed to know, and she asked about Rocco's favorite treats, since questions about the twins seemed to be difficult for him. She wasn't sure why, but she was hesitant to press too hard. For now, anyway. When the opportunity came again, she'd ask for more info and hope that now that the ice was broken, so to speak, he would feel comfortable filling her in on the details.

They arrived outside her apartment door. London turned to face Cooper, and her pulse went into overdrive. Would he kiss her? Did she *want* him to kiss her? It had been a great night but it wasn't, technically, a date. Was it? "Thank you for dinner. I had a wonderful time."

"You're welcome. I did, too. Thank you for letting me work, and keeping an eye out for Rocco. I wouldn't be surprised if he shows up again if he manages to make a break for it."

"It's not a problem. I'll let you know if he does." She pulled her keys from her bag, but her trembling fingers dropped them. London and Cooper moved at the same time, but she managed to stop herself and allowed him to retrieve them, thereby avoiding an even more awkward and potentially mortifying head bump.

"Thanks," she murmured when he straightened.

In the shift to get out of his way, she found her back pressed against the door. Cooper's eyes glittered as he reached out to grasp her hand in his and pressed the keys into her palm. He maintained his hold on her and lifted his now empty hand to brush an errant, windblown strand backward, toward her ear. That done, he lightly touched her earring before his fingers lowered to the skin bared by the off-shoulder top.

Cooper's fingers left a trail of fire, and her breath caught at the intensity. This was definitely something she wasn't used to. This… tangle of intrigue and interest and curiosity.

Seconds passed. Cooper met her gaze and held it a long moment before he inhaled, lowered his hand, and stepped away. "Good night, London. Sweet dreams."

Chapter 6

Cooper let himself into the house as quietly as possible and moved through the dimly lit interior toward his bedroom. The home's third-floor master suite was exclusively his home office since the larger bedroom had all the space needed for filing cabinets, digital storage and backups, monitors, a wall of progress and project boards, desk and conference table, a sitting area, and the like.

The second floor featured the kitchen, living area, and three bedrooms. The twins shared one bedroom for the time being, and Michelle the largest suite on that level. It had just made sense to give the nanny the second floor so she'd be close to the twins and still have privacy, allowing him privacy either in his office or in the lower-level efficiency-style apartment by the garage he'd taken for his own since it made it easy for him to come and go as needed.

Cooper dropped his keys in the bowl on the entry table and heard a sharp inhalation. He looked up to see Michelle wearing only a T-shirt that ended at the tops of her thighs. She was perfectly covered and decent considering less was worn on the beach, but it was still a shock to see his nanny in the state she was in.

"I didn't hear you come in."

"I didn't mean to startle you. What are you doing down here?"

"I-I was just… um"—she glanced toward his bedroom door—"checking on Rocco. He got upset when you left and… he was barking. I didn't want him waking the kids."

Michelle bit her lower lip and padded a few more steps toward him, rather than remain at the elevator door adjacent to his bedroom.

She paused within a few feet of him, her bare legs gleaming in the light.

"Do you, um, need anything?" She lifted her hand and smoothed it over her long, straight hair, blinking up at him. "Would you like a drink? I could get us something. We could watch some TV if you like."

"No, thanks."

"Are you sure?"

Decidedly uncomfortable, he cleared his throat and took a step back, disguising the move by pulling his phone from his rear pocket. "Yeah. You go upstairs and enjoy yourself."

"I wouldn't mind company. Just saying."

"I have work to do. Good night, Michelle." Cooper watched as she hesitated but finally turned and chose to take the stairs, every step giving him an eye-popping view of her long, bare legs. Was it his imagination or was there a little more sway to her barely covered hips?

Because she wants you to watch.

He forced himself to look away and quickly move to his apartment in case she had any doubt as to whether or not she had an audience. Michelle was quickly becoming an issue that had to be addressed, but for now, he wanted to see if he could get a few more hours of coding in as he wound down from the day and processed the evening with London.

He entered his bedroom and emptied his pockets of change and his wallet, and Rocco greeted him after leaving his position on the couch. After a few pats and ear rubs, Cooper sat on the edge of his bed to toe off his shoes and frowned when the bed felt warm. "Rocco? You been napping up here while I'm gone?"

Rocco sat on his haunches and stared at him, tongue hanging out of his mouth. Had Rocco moved from the bed to the couch before he'd walked in?

"Uh-huh." He put his shoes behind the couch for tidiness and headed back across the floor. In the two-story foyer, he opened the elevator door but paused. He could hear the television on the second level, and once again, he wondered what he was going to do about Michelle's behavior. Was he getting signals crossed? Thinking it flirting when she was just being... friendly? Maybe if he simply ignored her, she'd give up?

He led the way onto the elevator with Rocco following for the ride upstairs. He could have taken the stairs, but he didn't want to risk another encounter with Michelle. But shouldn't it tell him something if he was avoiding the nanny in his employ?

The elevator arrived on the third floor, and Cooper unlocked the door with a press of the ten-digit key code. He took his clients' privacy and security seriously.

As he settled himself in his desk chair, the night replayed in his mind.

Rocco head-butted Cooper's hand a time or two and sniffed. Cooper palmed the dog's head and scratched, grateful for the distraction. "Hey, bud. Yeah, you smell

London, don't you? You like her? That why you keep going back?"

He scratched Rocco's soft head, mind drifting. "I don't blame you. She's smart, funny. Beautiful," he said to the dog. "Comes from a great family from the sounds of it. All the more reason for her to steer clear of the crazy in this house, huh? I mean, there's an awful lot of evidence that Daria was right. No one in their right mind would want to take us on." He lowered his voice. "Kids, crazy, or flirtatious nanny," he said, shaking his head. "No wife or girlfriend would put up with that."

Rocco blinked and whined softly, his expression sorrowful.

Cooper released Rocco after another lengthy pat and gently pushed the dog away to unlock his computer. A quick search about his dinner companion revealed five-star reviews of London's Lattes with numerous comments about the beautiful owner.

The search also brought up images of her family via social media, along with newspaper articles featuring her family's various involvements in the community, none of which had anything to do with DUIs, drugs, thefts, or arrests. Cooper stared at the photos, mostly of London, but also her sisters, listed by their unusual names.

All five women were beautiful, seemingly happy. But why wouldn't they be? Maybe life hadn't turned out perfect for them, but when childhood wasn't a horror show full of suck, the odds were a little more favorable for a decent outcome.

Cooper sighed and ran his hand over his mouth and chin, remembering the way London had looked sitting across from him at the table. The conversation tonight had been engaging. London lit up a room when she entered, and it was obvious the locals thought a lot of her given the reactions she'd received as they'd entered the restaurant and walked along the pier.

By London's own words, her family was very involved in her life. Dinner had been fun. More fun than he'd had in months. Longer, considering the months before the breakup had been spent fighting with Daria over his decision to take in the twins.

He knew numbers. Statistics. And London's loving, stable background versus his chaotic, dysfunctional one would never mesh. She was the type of woman who'd want more. The white picket fence in front of a beach house, more kids. Involvement with her family, which he had no clue how to do. She'd need more than he knew how to give. More than he knew how to be.

He groaned and sat back in his chair.

Enough. Fantasies wouldn't get the work done. Wouldn't provide for the children now in his care. And that was priority number one.

Dating London?

If anything, tonight had proven without a doubt that wasn't going to happen.

EARLY THE FOLLOWING MORNING, London woke up to a bevy of texts from Carolina. She'd turned on her Do Not Disturb during the walk home and had gone straight to bed once she'd managed to get her quivering legs moving after Cooper's unusual goodbye.

But now?

Two missed phone calls and sixty-two texts. Carolina had resorted to texting the alphabet one letter at a time, something the sisters had started doing to demand a response when texts weren't returned fast enough, and then backwards, which made up fifty-two of the texts received. The other ten were demands for details. Multiple *helllllllos*, and one threat of bodily harm if London didn't respond.

Carolina was nothing if not persistent.

Still, London didn't have a slew of calls and texts from the *rest* of her family, which meant Caro had managed to keep her mouth shut about spotting them leaving the pier house. A small reprieve, if nothing else, but she'd better talk to Carolina soon or all bets were off.

They'd been seen by others. Walking down the streets, in the restaurant, on the pier. If her family hadn't already heard about her dinner out last night, they would soon. Such was life in a fishbowl—otherwise known as an island.

"It's about time."

London jumped at the sound of the voice coming from the darkened interior of the coffeehouse. She'd just left the private interior stairwell leading up to her apartment and was about to hit the lights when Carolina spoke. "Yeah, I'm going to need that spare key back. Like, now."

"Nope," Carolina grumbled from where she pushed herself up from the couch lining the far wall.

"You slept here?"

"Well, I wouldn't call what I did sleeping, but yeah. I mean, my shift at the pier house lasted until two because I covered for one of the guys, but I came straight here because I knew it would only be a few hours before you came down."

"Why didn't you just come up?"

"Because maybe you weren't alone?"

London immediately set to work brewing the first round for the day and shook her head at her sister's words. "You know I don't do that."

"I know you don't, but when you didn't answer *any* of

my texts—"

"You thought I brought him home and *slept* with him?"

"Hey, we always know when one of us is dating some-one, but *you've* been keeping secrets."

"No, I haven't. I'm not dating anyone," she said in response to Carolina's look of disbelief. "I only just met the man. And it wasn't a date. It was a thank-you dinner."

"You were dressed for a date. And lookin' hot, by the way—I wanna borrow that top sometime. He was hot, too. You made quite the fetching couple, and I wasn't the only one who noticed. Good on ya, mate."

"Will you stop with the Australianisms?"

"Hey, I have to practice so I fit in when I finally save up enough money to visit. And stop changing the subject. We're talking about you," Carolina said, the *you* emerging on a yawn and lasting several syllables.

"You should go home to Holland's and go to bed."

"I don't want to wake everyone up when they'll have to get up in a few hours anyway. For a kid, Samuel sure is a light sleeper," she said, referring to their nephew.

Ever since the hurricane had damaged Carolina's tiny apartment in the pier house attic, she'd been living at Holland's house with Holland, Ireland, and Ireland's son, Samuel. With Holland's heavy travel schedule and London's and Carolina's work schedules, the house was mainly used for sleeping when time allowed. "How are Ireland and Dominic doing?"

"I'll tell you after you tell me who hunky-hunk was."

"Who?" she said, hiding a grin at Caro's exasperated sputter. "Okay, okay. Fine. He's Rocco's owner."

"Rocco… that sweet dog that showed up here for a while? He's back?"

"Yes. He came in yesterday, and this time when I called the number on his collar, his owner came to retrieve him."

"Oh, man. Sweet dog *and* hot owner. Win-win."

"You're making more of it than it is. Cooper took me to dinner to say thank you for watching out for Rocco. That's *all*."

"Mm-hmm."

"Well, it is."

"So when are you going out again? What does he do? Where does he live?"

"I don't know—times three. Wait, I do know one of them. He's a software engineer. But I don't know the rest. He lives close, though, because he walked Rocco home last night and came back here within minutes while I changed out of my work clothes."

"Well, that definitely narrows down the search grid."

London paused during the process of inserting a fresh filter into one of the many machines. "Don't you dare go stalking him."

"Who, me?" Carolina said innocently. A little *too* innocently. Oh, this wasn't good.

A knock alerted her to her scheduled delivery, and London moved across the floor to unlock and open the door. "Hey, Marcus."

"Good morning, Miss London. How you doing today?"

"I'm fine."

"She had a date," Caro said from behind her.

"Oh, yeah? Who's the lucky guy?"

London took the tray of goodies from the deliveryman and shook her head. "No one. It wasn't a date. Will you hush?" she said to Carolina.

"Dinner," Carolina said to Marcus. "And she looked hot."

The older man chuckled at Carolina's description and gathered the tray from yesterday's delivery off of the table where she'd placed it last night after closing.

"Well, either way, he's a lucky man. You girls have a good day."

"You, too, Marcus."

"Bye, Marcus."

London balanced the tray against her side and flipped the lock back into position before carting it over to the counter where Carolina now sat. Her sister slumped against the bar like she'd pulled an all-nighter, leaning heavily to one side. "Please don't make a big deal out of a simple dinner. Ignore the fact you saw us, go home, and get some sleep."

"I will. Soon. Was he a good kisser?"

London busied herself with uncovering the tray of goodies and placing them in the display and tried not to see the images floating through her mind at the question. "It wasn't a date, so I wouldn't know."

"He didn't kiss you?"

Caro sounded so incredulous that London couldn't help but get defensive. He hadn't kissed her, and even though she wasn't certain it was a date, it had certainly felt like a date but then… "No. I told you, he was just saying thank you for watching out for Rocco and accidentally keeping me here past closing while he worked."

"Did you want him to kiss you?"

Oooh, Carolina just had to ask *that* question, didn't she? "I…"

"You *did*! You *like* him."

"I don't know him well enough to know if I like him. He was just… interesting."

"And hot."

"We had a nice time."

"And he's hot."

"It's not all about looks, you know. Stop being so shallow."

"I know it's not all about looks, but let's face it—when it comes to first impressions, what are they usually of? Hmm? Someone's looks. They might not be *all* that matter but they definitely do factor in. Besides, you wanted him to kiss you. Be honest."

"Fine. I wouldn't have run away if he had. Happy now? I admit it." Caro grinned at London from across the counter and London rolled her eyes. "For someone who didn't get a lot of sleep, you seem inordinately chatty."

"Because I'm happy for you. When *was* your last date?"

London gave her baby sister a death glare. "It is way too early in the morning for us to go there."

"Oh, my… Sorry. I forgot about Mr. Ego Pants."

Too bad she couldn't forget. Her evening out had been memorable only in how *un*memorable and boring it had been. The guy had spent the entire night talking about himself and how important he was. He'd told her about his car collection, his book of business, how he owned this property and that whatever. He'd traveled the world, held multiple jobs and positions. The seemingly nice guy had been so full of himself she'd sent the emergency code to Carolina from the bathroom, and within five minutes, Carolina had called, needing her to come quick, thereby ending the torturous night.

But last night? Cooper had seemed determined to keep *her* talking, and he'd listened to every word, like he'd been fascinated by the stories of her family's antics. He'd asked questions and kept asking them as though he hadn't been able to know enough. Like he was interested on a more personal level— that is, until it was time to say good night. Maybe a truly old-fashioned gentleman wouldn't have tried to kiss her on a first date, but he could've kissed her cheek. Right?

"So he really didn't kiss you?"

"Caro, I think I would remember if he had. No, he... I dropped my keys and he picked them up for me and we were standing super close, but instead of a kiss, he"—she brought her hand up and mimicked Cooper's actions from last night—"brushed his knuckles against my earring and then stroked his fingers over my shoulder for a second or two and then... he said good night and walked away."

Silence followed her statement, and London's gaze shifted to where Carolina sat watching her. Her tired, sleepy sister had sat up on the barstool and now stared at her with wide eyes that no longer held the slightest bit of fatigue.

"Wow."

"I know. It was so—"

"*Weird.* Or sweet. I'm not sure which."

London crossed her arms over her chest and frowned at Caro.

She knew which it was. And it definitely *hadn't* been weird. Cooper's brief touch had left her trembling and breathless—something she didn't remember ever feeling before. "Go home," she ordered again. "Or go upstairs and climb into my bed so I can get to work and not play Twenty Questions."

Carolina slid off the stool and gathered the backpack-style purse she'd used as a pillow and had carried with her from the couch to the bar.

"Okay, okay. I'm going. But next time introduce me to *Cooper* or I'll send out the Bat signal and you'll have us all appear to meet your date."

London followed Carolina to the door leading upstairs to her apartment and leaned against the doorframe as Carolina began climbing the stairs, her backpack bouncing at her side with every step. "Oh, for the love of— It wasn't a *date!*"

Chapter 7

Several weeks passed after that evening out, and Cooper's biggest regret in regard to his dinner with London was not kissing her when he'd had the chance.

He'd plucked up her keys and stood so close all he'd had to do was lean in and… He didn't think she would've rejected him. But even at that early stage of their friendship, logic had reared its ugly head and told him a woman like London would steer clear of him once she knew all there was to know. That awareness left him with the reality that he didn't want to ruin a good thing, and he also didn't have the time or the energy to invest in something that wasn't going to end well.

He had too much work to do, too many projects scheduled, a business to run, and the kids to consider. Throwing a high-risk personal relationship into the balancing act wasn't worth the long shot of it actually succeeding. Like London had said, he liked order and schedules, and if he was going to invest in a relationship, he wanted to feel like it would work.

Cooper groaned and ran his hands over his face. His

focus had to be on work, the future. Ballet and soccer, baseball and cheerleading. College or trade school. Whatever the twins did, it would cost him, and he had to have a plan and way to provide. That plan also had to include stability, and the only way to guarantee that was to not allow someone in their lives who could potentially leave when things got tough. And given the twins' background, things could. Would?

He had to be realistic.

Cooper had gone back to the coffee shop to work a few times since that first day as though he'd only ever considered that evening a thank-you dinner as he'd said, but not a day passed that the memory of stroking his fingers over London's bare shoulder didn't fill his head and make him crave more. Crave her.

London probably thought him a creep, especially given the touch and lack of pursuit since, but he'd needed something to carry with him. The scent of her, the feel of her. The look of her staring up at him with her blue-green eyes and parted lips that was something out of a fantasy. And his reach.

Whenever temptation overtook him and he opened his mouth to recklessly broach the subject of a real date, however, he managed to shut himself down. Remember all that she'd told him about her life versus the reality of his. He had the twins' best interests to protect. Their future. And that meant protecting himself. Keeping his head straight and focused on work instead of setting himself up to get dumped again. It amazed him how complicated life could get when all he craved was simplicity, but daily survival wasn't something to dismiss.

Bella's scream from the living room below ripped through Cooper's thoughts and shattered what little was left of his concentration.

He'd put off leaving for the coffee shop today because of the growing tension and awareness he felt as each day passed. It was getting harder and harder for him to just sit there and act like a friend when he desired more. He and London made small talk. Exchanged smiles. And every day, she inevitably caught him watching her at various times because he wasn't able to keep his eyes off of her.

She hadn't questioned his about-face after their wonderful evening, but one day, his gut told him if things kept on as they were, she would. So why continue to go there? Why do that to her? To himself? What was he hoping to accomplish?

Rocco paced across the floor in front of the closed home office door like he had the last fifteen minutes or so, unable to settle because, whenever he did, one of the twins let loose and sent the dog on high alert once more. "Roc."

The call brought Rocco to Cooper in an instant, and he stroked the golden's head. "If I let you out, you'll just go down there and get attacked by them." *We both will.*

Though his attacker would more than likely be the nanny. This morning when he'd returned from his beach run and used the outdoor shower to rinse off the sand, he'd emerged to find Michelle waiting for him with a towel, water bottle, and a seductive expression that swept him from head to toe and couldn't be misinterpreted. All while the twins rode their play toys on the concrete a few feet away.

His gut told him he needed to hire new childcare but when? How? He was in the final stages of this project, and the deadline loomed over him like an anvil. He had no time to waste due to the next project scheduled to begin right behind it. Now was not a good time to rock the boat by adding childcare interviews into the mix.

Rocco whined and nudged Cooper's leg with his head.

"If you go outside, you're going to jump the fence, aren't you?"

Rocco sat on his haunches and looked at Cooper with what could only be described as a hopeful expression at the mention of going *out*.

He'd discovered Rocco's escape route after a look around the yard. One of the moving men had placed an outdoor storage bin too close to the fence, and Rocco had apparently been using it as a launch pad. Still, the dog was too smart for his own good, and if there was a way out, Cooper knew Rocco would find it. "Sorry I had to ruin your fun, but what if you got picked up by Animal Control, huh? Then what?"

Rocco blinked at him and whined again.

In the other part of the house, Cooper heard the heavier footfalls of Michelle as she raced across the room. Cooper held his breath and, sure enough, a thump sounded, followed by Bella's shrill cry. Ash had never been the queen of coordination and Bella seemed to have her mother's penchant for mishaps.

Rocco released yet another low whine, and Cooper sat forward in his chair, elbows braced on his knees as he cradled the dog's big head. "Okay, you win. Let's go see her." Cooper refused to consider whether the "her" was London or Rocco's little Rosie, but either way it didn't matter. Sensing the win, Rocco jumped up in the air, tail wagging and doggie smile in place.

Maybe he should feel guilty about leaving Michelle to handle the twins on her own so much, but he paid her well, really well, and when it came to knowing what the twins needed, the young woman had it together, even if she was off the mark on keeping things professional and not flirting with her boss.

Cooper gathered up his things while Rocco spun in

circles in his excitement and paused every few spins to check on his human's progress.

He opened the office door and allowed Rocco to run ahead down the stairs. The doggie door was still fastened from last night, so Roc wouldn't be going anywhere without him, even if Roc could jump the baby gate protecting the kids from the stairs.

As he entered the living room, he noticed Michelle wiped Harry's mouth with a rag before she quickly moved toward the kitchen. She had her back to him as she placed something in the cabinet and shut the door before turning to face him.

"Hey, I was about to come find you. What would you like for lunch?" she asked.

Something about her tone gave him pause, but he shook his head and pulled Rocco's leash off of the hook. "I'm heading out to the coffee shop to work. I'm in the completion stage and the time crunch is kicking in."

"Oh, okay."

He narrowed his gaze on her. Something seemed… off. The kids had been fairly wild all morning, running, screaming, and generally being kids. "Are you going to be okay with them?"

"Of course. Don't be silly. We'll be fine."

The young woman flashed him a bright smile. Cooper looked away and glanced at the twins, noticing that Bella had a red stain on her shirt. "Popsicles already today?"

He didn't want them to have too much sugar. His mother had a tendency to soothe every ache, pain, or problem with food, and during the brief period of time she'd had full custody of the kids, she'd fed them cheap, high-sugar, high-fat foods. He was okay with a little here and there, but he didn't want Michelle making it a thing just to keep them quiet.

"Just a little watered-down juice after she choked on her oatmeal."

He nodded his understanding and leashed Rocco, who waited patiently at his feet. "Call if something comes up."

"Of course."

Cooper headed toward the door only to change directions and cut through the laundry room toward the back, where the extra dog bags were kept. He grabbed a roll and set his computer bag atop the dryer to put the roll into the water bottle netting on the side when his gaze spotted what looked to be his favorite T-shirt in… Michelle's laundry?

Maybe she'd seen it in the hamper and decided to wash it?

But… wait, was that the T-shirt she'd had on the night of his dinner with London? He tried to remember the last time he'd worn the shirt and couldn't.

Cooper turned to go back to the kitchen when Rocco whined and moved toward the door, circling like he needed to go out.

Cooper sighed and shook his head. He'd ask Michelle about the shirt later. Right now he had to walk a dog and meet a deadline. Everything else had to wait.

TWENTY MINUTES LATER, Cooper walked into London's Lattes with Rocco on a leash and his laptop hanging at his side.

"Um, hi, Cooper."

Two women whipped around at the sound of London's greeting, and given their similarities to London and his internet search after their dinner, he knew was looking at one of her sisters and mother. "Ladies," he said simply.

Rocco gave London a tail-wagging greeting, and

Cooper watched as she smiled at the dog and slipped him a treat from the pocket of her apron.

"Oh, sorry. Habit. I should've asked first."

"It's fine. He doesn't get a lot of treats at home because he cleans up whatever the kids drop."

"Kids?" the older of the two women asked.

"My niece and nephew," he murmured.

"They're three," London said. "Almost four?"

He nodded.

"Twins?"

London shot the women a look Cooper easily interpreted as urging them to mind their manners and not get too nosy. She'd asked about the twins in general terms over the last couple of weeks, but he'd never quite gotten around to discussing how he'd wound up with them. It wasn't a subject he liked to dwell on, but he supposed he'd have to come up with some sort of socially acceptable story. The truth and yet... not. Just for occasions such as this. "Yes. A boy and a girl."

"Oh, how fun! Wait. This is Rocco," the older woman said, a pleased smile forming on her lips as she apparently made the connection.

Cooper leaned down and released the golden, and Rocco immediately hurried to Rosie's bed and settled in beside his friend after a few sniffs and excited-to-see-her circles.

"It is," London said. "Rocco and his family moved to town a little while ago. Mom, this is Cooper Bale. Cooper, my mom, Andrea, and my sister Ireland."

"Ladies, it's a pleasure to meet you." London resembled her mother. They both had delicate, angled faces, bright green eyes. Andrea's hair had changed from London's medium brown to mostly gray, but the woman carried the change well and was quite striking as a result. It didn't take a lot of imagination to see London thirty years in the future.

"Cooper, can I get you some coffee? Your usual?"

"I'd like that."

"What's your order, Cooper? So I'll know, in case he comes into the inn," Ireland said to her sister.

"Uh, black."

"Uh-oh."

"Stop it," London muttered from behind the counter.

"Cooper, how do you like our little island?"

"Mom, don't badger my customers."

He laughed at London's gentle reprimand and nodded. "I like it a lot, especially now that we've gotten a little more squared away at the house."

"And where's home?"

"Mom."

"Forgive the intrusion, Cooper, but we like to know our neighbors."

He winked at London and enjoyed the flush it put on her cheeks way too much. "I don't mind, ma'am. I'm on Fifth, almost directly behind the coffee shop. It's the only blue house on the street."

"I'm familiar. That's a beautiful home. It's just you then, when the children aren't visiting?"

"Mom, will you give the man a break?"

Cooper shifted his weight from foot to foot and glanced around the interior. The coffee shop held three other people besides the Cohen women, and none of them seemed to be paying any attention to their conversion. But he knew in small towns—islands—that wasn't typically the case. But since it was as good a time as any to inform everyone of the reality of his living situation… "No, ma'am. Actually, I have custody of the twins, so it's the three of us, plus a live-in nanny."

"I see," Andrea murmured. "That's quite the load to carry as a single man."

"Which is *why* Cooper probably needs to put that laptop to work, am I right?" London interjected in a cheerful tone from behind the counter. "Cooper, run while you can. I'll block your exit and bring your order."

"Oh, London," her mother said, tone scolding and seemingly a little embarrassed.

He chuckled, but it sounded strained to his own ears. "It's fine. But London is right. I do need to get to work. I have a deadline and a lot to get done. London, would you care to add a breakfast sandwich to the order? The egg white one," he said, pointing to one in the case.

"Sure thing."

"It was nice to meet you, ladies."

"We've enjoyed meeting you," Andrea said. "Rocco is such a dear."

"Thanks. He was top of his class in obedience school, so it's nice to hear the training paid off."

"Don't worry, Mom, you'll undoubtedly see Cooper again. He's been coming here periodically to work," Ireland said.

"Oh, really?"

Andrea gave Cooper a knowing smile every matchmaking mama seemed to have conquered. Too bad she'd change her mind if she knew his history. "Uh, yes, ma'am. The deadline," he said again, hoping the woman wouldn't take offense. "My home office isn't as quiet as it used to be."

"I'm sure it isn't. Well, I look forward to seeing you again soon."

He nodded. "Enjoy your day."

Cooper turned and made his way across the room to a

table tucked into the far corner and lowered his backpack onto the surface.

London appeared behind him, his coffee order in hand.

"I'm *so* sorry," she murmured.

"No problem."

"I'd like to say it's an isolated incident, but Carolina Cove is a small town *and* an island, so it's a double whammy on the get-to-know-your-neighborness. I did warn you."

He glanced over her head to where her sister and mother sat and found them eyeing him as London set his coffee on the table. "So you did. Thanks for bringing this over."

"Not a problem. I'll bring the sandwich out as soon as it's ready."

"Thanks."

London hesitated, opened her mouth as though wanting to say something else, but closed it and turned to head back to the counter where her family waited. Cooper watched her go, looking away only to lock gazes with Andrea, who gave him a feminine, narrow-eyed glance he also associated with mamas the world over.

She knew he was interested in her daughter.

But like him, Andrea Cohen wasn't sure what to make of it.

Chapter 8

London walked back to where her mom and sister sat at the bar and tried to ignore the way they both watched her as she set to work fixing Cooper's breakfast sandwich order. "Stop. Both of you. Right now," she ordered when they ignored her. "You're being so obvious."

"He's *very* handsome," her mother said. "Can't seem to take his eyes off of you, either."

"You're totally imagining that."

"Did you flirt with him?"

"*Mom.*"

"I'm just saying…"

"Mom, I mean it. He'll *hear* you."

Andrea waved a hand in the air as though waving away the words, shifted forward on her stool, and lowered her voice.

"You've always been so bashful," her mother said. "He's interested. You should *flirt*."

London met Ireland's gaze and watched as her sister lifted her hands as though in surrender. London sighed. No help there. *Traitor.* "Ireland just got engaged. Let's focus on that, shall we?"

This was Ireland's second engagement, would be her second marriage. Whereas London had yet to be asked. She'd come close once. Well, maybe. At least she'd *thought* her boyfriend at the time was going to ask, but when she'd surprised him with a birthday breakfast and caught him in bed with his coworker, well, that had ended that.

"Yeah, let's," Ireland agreed. "And I'd like to reiterate that the key words to remember when it comes to planning are *small* and *intimate*. It's a second wedding for both of us, and we don't want too much fuss. Understood?"

When Ireland and London simultaneously looked at their mama, Andrea sat back on the barstool with an offended expression.

"Can't I have any fun?"

Ireland focused on London.

"That's mother speak for over-the-top insane and more than we want. Londy, will you please handle the engagement party?"

"But… *no*," Mama said. "No, I've already called several venues this morning, and—"

"Of course I will," London agreed. "We can have the engagement party here and keep it super casual."

"*Perfect.*"

"Girls—"

"Mama, it's decided. London can handle the engagement party, and you and I will plan a *small* wedding on the beach come spring. Or early summer. We haven't decided yet since Dominic is still trying to get things sorted out at work."

Ireland's fiancé was an Atlanta attorney who'd spent the last few months dividing his time between locations. And while London was curious as to where the two would eventually call home, she knew better than to ask in front of their mama.

London watched as her mother propped both elbows on the counter in front of her, looking much like a child who'd just had her balloon deflate.

"Should I be grateful you're not eloping somewhere?"

"Yes, because we discussed it."

London couldn't stop the laugh that emerged and quickly held up her hands in surrender. "Sorry. It slipped."

"Mama, all of your big plans are going to have to wait on someone's *first* wedding. I did that once. I don't need it again. It's someone else's turn."

"You girls just wait. When you have daughters of your own, you'll see, and you'll be disappointed when you don't get to make a fuss."

"I know, Mama, but Dominic and I agreed to keep things small. All of the planning is such a waste of time any—"

"Oh! Speaking of time…" Her mother gathered up her purse after a quick check of her watch. "I told your father I'd be back in an hour and that was nearly two hours ago. I was just so excited when you called to tell me this morning."

Mama quickly hugged them both before rushing toward the door, pausing briefly to say her goodbyes to Cooper before she went racing out.

London watched her mother depart before shifting her attention back to Ireland. Her sister's expression had gone pensive and seemed a million miles away. London frowned. "Hey. What's that look about? Everything okay?"

"What? Oh, yeah," Ireland said. "It's just Mama's right about one thing."

"What's that?"

"Londy, we can't wait to have another baby—hopefully a

little girl—which means the longer it takes for this wedding to happen, the longer it will be before *that* happens. Maybe Dominic and I should elope?"

"Mama would flip."

"I *know*. Now go give the man his sandwich so we can talk."

London quickly finished the order and grabbed rolled utensils. She delivered Cooper's order with a smile but didn't linger since his headphones were in place and he typed at record speed.

The moment she stepped back behind the counter within hearing distance, Ireland sighed.

"I'm just so ready."

"For?"

"Everything. I feel like I haven't enjoyed life in ages and I'm ready to. Dominic is wonderful. I mean really wonderful. After the divorce, I honestly never thought I would feel this way again. That I could ever find love again or be so happy. Appreciate so much. Little, inconsequential things. Now… every moment is precious and I see things differently so… why wait? Especially when Dominic doesn't want to wait either."

"I'm sure you're excited, but it's wise not to rush. Just enjoy this time."

"I guess."

Ireland took a sip of her latte before leveling a stare at London.

"So, you had a date with Cooper?"

"What? No. We're… friends. He's a customer."

"A friend is always a good thing, as are customers, but that wasn't what I asked."

London sucked in a breath. "That little snitch."

Ireland laughed softly. "Don't be upset. Caro was *so* excited for you. She came home as I was leaving that morning and looked ready to burst. I think she would've if she'd kept it a secret."

"That may be so, but that night wasn't a date and she shouldn't have said anything," London said quietly, embarrassed by the fact everyone knew about the dinner and yet things hadn't progressed further. Maybe most people wouldn't care, but her sisters and mother would wonder why and… It *was* embarrassing and she wondered what was wrong with her.

"Too late for that now," Ireland said. "The question is whether you wanted it to be a date?"

London glanced over Ireland's shoulder to where Cooper sat working, grateful the headphones were in place. "I… wouldn't have minded."

"You like him."

"It doesn't matter."

"It does matter. You *like* him."

"Well, obviously he *doesn't* like me. He's been in here nearly every day since and hasn't said a word out of turn or acted interested, so… problem solved," she said, lifting her shoulders in a forlorn shrug.

"Did you clash on politics? World views? Faith?"

"No. Nothing. At least, nothing I can think of. He asked me a lot of questions and seemed to have a nice time."

"What about him? Did you ask him questions? Make it clear *you're* interested?"

London shifted and leaned more heavily against the counter after two of her customers waved goodbye and made their way out the door. She was hyperaware of the fact only Cooper and London remained, and the last thing she wanted was for him to hear them discussing him. Thankfully Cooper seemed wholly focused on his task. Still, she made sure to keep her voice to a whisper. "I tried to ask questions, but he would usually steer the conversation back to me and our family. He wanted to know about my childhood and you guys and... He seemed fine at the time, but obviously something turned him off."

"Or maybe he's just super busy with that deadline of his and he doesn't want to start something he can't dedicate the proper time and attention to. Some guys are like that."

"Maybe." Could that be it? He did seem to be under the gun, so to speak, when it came to work. And he'd just moved and had the twins at home. Maybe... that was it? Because prideful or not, he *did* look at her in a way that seemed like he liked her, too. Was interested but holding back.

"Rocco, hey, boy. How are you?"

London looked up to find Dally had entered the coffee shop. Rocco rose from his position on the floor and tail-wagged his way to greet the familiar man. It wasn't until Dally had made it nearly to the counter that the older man stopped in his tracks. "Dally? Are you all right?"

The man lost what little color he had in his pale complexion.

Rocco barked and sat at Dally's feet, tail sweeping the floor as he stared up at the man. Rocco's bark and race across the floor had gained Cooper's attention, and London watched as he removed the headphones and turned to see what was going on, swiveling up and out of his chair in a surge of movement that sent Rocco scurrying about excitedly.

London's stomach tightened in a knot at the visible tension between the two men. All of a sudden the pieces clicked, and she gasped.

"What? What's going on?" Ireland asked in a low voice.

"Hey—Scout... it's good see you."

Cooper glared at Dally, the muscles of his face drawn tight.

"Wish I could say the same. And don't call me that."

"It's just a nickname, son—"

"You do not have the right to call me that. Ever."

Cooper sent a glance in her direction before turning back to the table and shoving his laptop and other items in his backpack as fast as he could. He called Rocco to his side and leashed the dog.

"Cooper—"

"I don't know how you met him," Cooper said with a jerk of his head toward Dally, "but you'd best stay away. For your own sake."

"Cooper, D-Dally's been nothing but kind."

A rough laugh emerged from Cooper's chest. "Yeah… Still can't say the same." He slung the backpack onto his shoulder before pointing a finger at Dally. "You stay away from me. From *us*. You got that? And if you have any care for London, you'll stay away from her, too."

The silence that followed Cooper's departure lengthened for long moments before London moved from behind the counter to Dally's side. The older man wove on his feet, completely ashen. "Dally, sit down."

"No. He's right. I'm no good. Wasn't— I should go."

"Not until you're more yourself again. Come on, sit down," London ordered, leading him to the closest chair.

Ireland set a water bottle in front of him.

"You don't look well."

"I'm f-fine."

"Dally… you're Cooper's *father*?"

The man's eyes filled with tears. He nodded but then just as quickly shook his head. He pulled something from his pocket and held it, rubbing his thumbs over the surface repeatedly.

"Yes. No… He's right. I lost the right to be called that a long time ago."

Ireland and London seated themselves on either side of the man, sensing his need for support. London wanted to go after Cooper, but she also felt he needed time to recover from the shock of seeing his father in her shop. "Talk to us, Dally. What on earth just happened? What was that all about?"

"Ah, girls. That's a story I'm too ashamed to tell."

"You need to tell someone," London murmured.

"S'pose I do," the man agreed, lifting a trembling fist to his face to roughly wipe away the moisture that had leaked from his eyes. "But not to you. I need… I need to go to a meeting."

London frowned at the words but Ireland stretched out a hand and placed it over Dally's. He dropped the item in his fist to grip Ireland's fingers and London saw a coin.

"There's one at a church off of Dow," Ireland said. "Near the fire station. I think it starts in about fifteen minutes. You should make it in plenty of time."

It took a moment. A long moment and another glance at the coin to finally understand what Dally meant by needing a meeting. An AA meeting. As quickly as that sank in came the knowledge and origin of Cooper's personality type as the child of an alcoholic. *Who has custody of his niece and nephew.*

Did that mean Cooper's sister was an alcoholic, too? Was that how Cooper was granted custody?

One by one the pieces began to fall into place.

"Do you want me to drive you?" Ireland offered.

"No, hon. I'm fine."

"Are you sure?"

"Yes. It was just a shock, though it shouldn't have been after seeing Rocco in here. I knew it would happen eventually. Hoped it would. But I just wasn't expecting it today, I guess."

"Dally, please… What happened between you and Cooper?" London caught Ireland's look of surprise that she'd ask such a personal question after Dally specifically saying he was embarrassed to say, but she couldn't help herself. Not after witnessing Cooper's response. The look on his face… the pain. Both Cooper and Dally were walking wounded, and it broke her heart.

"Maybe I'll tell you sometime. I need to get to that meeting for now." Dally stood, the chair legs scraping against the floor like razor blades on her nerves.

London and Ireland watched as the man left as quickly as Cooper had. Seconds passed and they sat there in silence.

"Wow."

"I know," London whispered. "I've gotten to know Dally from his visits here, and Cooper, but I never put the two of them together."

Ireland inhaled and crossed her arms over her front, hugging herself.

"We were blessed. I mean, Mom and Dad drank sometimes but never irresponsibly. At least not around us. It wasn't ever an issue."

London nodded. "It must have been bad, huh? For Cooper to have had that kind of reaction?"

Ireland met London's gaze and nodded.

"I'd say so."

But how bad was it? Given the reactions of both father and son, London was afraid to imagine. She inhaled and shoved herself away from the table, glad for the lack of customers. "I need a distraction. Let's… plan your party or something."

"Londy, that can wait. I can stay here if you want to go find Cooper. Check on him."

"No, I-I… I need to give him time. *I* need time to figure out what I should say. But I need to do something besides let *that* replay in my head," she said, waving a hand toward the spot where Dally and Cooper had stood ready to go to war. "You know?"

"Do you want to go after him?"

After seeing the look on Cooper's face? Getting to know him these last couple of weeks? "Of course I do. Not knowing what happened is killing me. But Cooper needs to be the one to decide. *If* he wants to talk and confide in me… Right?"

Chapter 9

Cooper spotted London the moment she left the bridge closest to the pier and descended the steps to the sand. She paused to remove her shoes and turned left, slowly walking in his general direction.

He'd like to think he had some kind of pull that drew her toward him, but he knew that was wishful thinking. Especially after what had happened in the coffee shop. Storming out hadn't been ideal. He should've ordered Dalton out of London's Lattes, but he'd been so blindsided by Dalton's appearance that he hadn't been able to get away fast enough. Teach a kid to run away at the first sign of trouble, and they tended to continue the pattern. He was embarrassed now, however, because he'd left London and Ireland behind to deal with the man.

The ocean breeze lifted London's loose hair from around her face and blew it all about. He watched how she walked, slow and easy, head down, shoulders back, toes in the sand and her thin flip-flops tucked into one of the rear pockets of her shorts.

She kept walking and he waited, watched. Wondered if

he was ready to have the conversation she'd probably expect if she spotted him. The conversation she deserved so she'd know without a doubt that he wasn't the man she needed in her life.

London must have sensed his gaze on her, because she turned her head in his direction. He knew the moment she saw him sitting on the sand, back in the shadows created by the dunes. She paused on the divide created by sun and dunes, and he felt her stare like a physical touch.

Would she keep walking? Join him?

The odds were fifty-fifty in his book.

After a moment, she squared her shoulders and lifted her chin and stepped fully into the shadows. Cooper prepared himself as best he could, but the next hour or so wasn't going to be an easy one.

After the confrontation with Dalton, Cooper had walked home long enough to stash Rocco in the house with Michelle and the twins and grab his keys. He'd forced himself to find another place to work and managed to compartmentalize his mind enough to finish the project that had taken so much of his time. He'd spent two hours testing and reviewing, then scheduled delivery of the package one full day ahead of deadline. Finishing the project didn't bring the sense of satisfaction it usually did, though, and the meeting with Dalton was wholly to blame.

"Hey."

Cooper lifted his head and found her bright green eyes studying him closely. She'd shoved her sunglasses atop her head, and now her eyebrows pinched above her nose in an adorable scrunch. "Hey, yourself."

"Mind if I join you?"

"Can't say I'm good company."

"Maybe talking will help."

Ah, but would it? How could talking to someone like

London, with her background and idyllic childhood, do anything but remind him of all reasons they wouldn't work?

She lowered herself onto the sand beside him, knees to chest, arms looped around her legs, and stared out at the ocean. "I... didn't know Dally was your father."

Dally. A curse almost left him before he stopped it. "He told you to call him that?"

She turned her head, cheek resting on her knees.

"Yeah. That's not his name?"

"That's what we— what Ash called him as a kid."

"Your sister?"

"Yeah. Ashley. She was nine years younger than me and, when she was a baby, kept getting Dalton and Daddy confused. It came out as Dally."

"I see."

London shifted on the sand, released her legs, and stretched them out in front of her before propping her hands behind her hips, head turned in his direction and that gaze of hers not letting up the heat.

"It seems like when we're together, I do all of the talking. I think that's been kind of deliberate on your part. So now I'm asking... Will you tell me about you? Please. I'd like to know more."

Cooper had braced himself for the questions but he still wasn't prepared. "You don't want to know, London. It's not something anyone wants to know."

"Tell me anyway."

Her words were almost carried away by the wind, drowned out by the squawk of the birds, but he heard them and knew even if he hadn't, she wasn't going to let up. The time had come. "Why? Why do you... care?"

She inhaled and shook her head so that the long braid fell over her shoulder, down her back.

"It's what friends do. They listen. Try to help if they can."

"Is that what we are? Friends?"

"Well, you've made it clear you don't want to be more."

"That's where you're wrong."

Her head whipped toward him, one of her eyebrows lifted high. Cooper watched the flashes of expression cross her face, fascinated by the play of muscle and insight. He saw speculation. Inquisitiveness. Doubt. It was the doubt that got him. "It can't be that surprising, London. You're beautiful, incredibly smart, insanely sexy. Who wouldn't be interested in you and want more?"

She blinked once, lips parting as though the words had sucked the air out of her lungs.

"But you've never… I don't understand, Cooper. If you truly feel that way, why haven't you said something? D-done something?"

"Because you may be curious about me now, but once you know everything there is to know about me, my history, you won't feel the same way."

"Why don't you let me decide? It's my choice, isn't it?"

Even though it was the last thing he wanted, he resigned himself to cutting the vein. "I guess it is. What do you want to know?"

"Everything."

He'd hoped for a little more time. Time to settle in and get into a routine with the twins, maybe pretend to be a normal family before she knew the dirty, dysfunctional details. "You know the basics. Software engineer. Single," he reiterated, earning a smile at the memory his words evoked. "And guardian of the twins. What you don't know is how it all came about. My sister, Ashley, died of an overdose. She tried to stay clean during the pregnancy, which was a miracle in itself, but she didn't always succeed. Afterwards… whether it was postpartum depression or an addict needing a fix, no one knows, but she… began using and the cycle started all over."

"I'm sorry."

"Me, too."

"Is that when you got custody? Their father…?"

The dirtier details. Not something he liked thinking about when it came to his baby sister. "I don't think she knew who the father was. She'd… do anything for a fix. But, no. He's not in the picture. When Ash passed away, my mother got custody of them and took care of them until earlier this year. The kids went a long way in helping her get over the pain of losing her only daughter."

The roar of the ocean faded away as his mind returned to that time, to the run-down house down an old dirt road in rural North Carolina. "But then she got sick. A cough she couldn't shake. She was gone in a matter of months."

"Oh, Cooper."

London's shock was evident in the way she breathed his name, the look of horror on her face.

"I don't know what to say. I am so sorry."

He loved his mother. He did. But when he mourned her, it wasn't that he mourned her loss as much as mourned who she could have been. Should have been. "Thank you. She was… She did the best she could."

London scooted closer, a deep frown marring her beautiful face.

"What do you mean?"

"She wasn't always stable herself—at least when it came to Dalton. She was— wasn't," he corrected, "strong. Neither was Ashley. Both were very codependent, both enablers."

"Keep going," she whispered.

He inhaled and exhaled and had to break eye contact

to focus on the story he told. "No matter how drunk Dalton would stay or how violent it got, Mom would take him back. Years went by but finally Dalton left for good. I was gone by then. I'd gotten that scholarship to college, but Ash was just a kid, watching it all like a bad rerun. I should've stayed or taken her with me—"

"You were a kid, Cooper. No legal agency would've allowed you to be Ashley's guardian."

The words brought comfort to a certain extent. Rationally he knew he couldn't have handled Ash, because when Dalton had left for good, Ashley was already acting out. Running with the wrong crowd, getting drunk, having sex. But if taking her could've somehow changed the course of events… "Once Mom got a diagnosis, it was only a matter of time because she'd waited so long. Anyway, she made me promise I wouldn't put the twins in foster care, and I agreed."

Cooper felt London staring at him, watching him, and he was curious as to her thoughts.

"It doesn't matter what I think, of course, but you're doing right by them," she said softly.

It mattered what she thought. More than she could ever know. "Am I?"

"Of course. You're their uncle. I'm assuming their only immediate relative other than… Dalton?"

He nodded.

"Do you doubt taking them in was the right thing to do?"

He stared into her green eyes and battled the ever-present fear he had that he'd screw the twins up as badly as he and Ashley had been screwed up. "I honestly don't know."

London's gaze narrowed on him and she shifted again, turning to fully face him.

"I can't imagine losing my mother and my sister *and* becoming a dad in such a short amount of time. I'm sure it's been overwhelming, but *of course* the twins are better off with you, Cooper. Why would you think otherwise?"

For the first time, he realized she hadn't run screaming down the beach at the level of dysfunction in the story, but... only time would tell if the brakes appeared and she began avoiding him or making excuses. "Something my ex-girlfriend said."

"Well, forget whatever it was," London ordered. "Cooper, I realize we don't know each other very well, but what I do know of you? You're dedicated, hardworking. Kind. I see you with Rocco and Rosie. Not only that, I see how they respond to you. Animals sense the bad in people and that's not something they sense in you."

"We all have a dark side, London. Maybe you just haven't seen mine yet." He said the words while sliding her a glance. "How do you know?"

"I don't. That's where trust and faith come in, but you have given me no reason to doubt what discernment tells me about you. One of the many things my dad taught me was to trust my gut and with you..."

"It's hard for me to understand how someone like you can want to be any part of the dysfunction I come from."

"Someone like me. Seriously?"

"Yeah."

"Cooper, that's a pretty big assumption you're making. Look, I can only imagine how bad things got in your child-hood, but you aren't your past. Are you harboring some deep, dark secret?"

A rough sound left his chest. A laugh, a huff, he wasn't sure which. "No."

"Okay, then."

"It's not that simple, London."

"Of course it isn't. But you've already broken the cycle. When you were that kid, did you want to be like your father, or something more?"

All of his life—from the moment he knew Dalton's drunkenness and abuse weren't *right*—he'd focused on getting out. Doing better. Being better. Whereas Ashley had had the mentality that it was a given part of her future no matter what. "More."

"Exactly. Because that's exactly what I see in you. The past is over, history."

"Not when Dalton's making a nuisance of himself."

"Cooper, I'm not taking up for Dally, but the man you're describing isn't the man I know."

"He's dangerous."

"Maybe he was. But now? I'm not so sure. There's something going on with him. Every time I see Dally, he looks worse than the time before."

"Drinking does that, London."

"Maybe. But today after you left he was adamant about getting to an AA meeting. He's sober."

"He's tried before. It doesn't stick." How many times had Dalton begged forgiveness, claiming to be clean, only to turn around and go on a bender?

Too many to count.

Too many times they'd let down their guard only to pay the price for it.

"Well, for what it's worth, the chip he carries has a number on it, and from what you've told me, I'm thinking the number is close to how many days it's been since your sister passed."

Was it possible? "He showed up at my mother's burial claiming he's been sober since Ash died. That the news had… changed him."

"You don't believe him?"

Cooper inhaled. "Given the number of times it's happened in the past, no."

London moved closer to him, until her knee touched the top of his thigh. Cooper stared at her face, taking in every detail from the light smattering of freckles across her nose and cheeks barely visible beneath her makeup to the shine on her lips. "I can't decide if you're real."

She blinked up at him. "What do you mean?"

"Do you really think our pasts don't matter?"

Her expression softened, her beautiful gaze holding his.

"I think we carry it with us always, but the key is using it for the lessons it teaches us, not as a punishment. That's how we become us, the person we're supposed to be."

"I don't want to be him, London. Ever."

London leaned toward him and placed her head on his bicep. He inhaled the scent of her hair and rested his chin atop her head. "That man destroyed anything good we ever had in our lives. He broke it, stole it, pawned it. He physically and verbally abused my mother until she wasn't a person, just a shell who tried to eat herself into oblivion to dull the pain. And Ash… she never stood a chance."

"That's where I disagree. You made choices to get where you are today. Just like Ashley made choices. She chose wrong."

"My ex said I was crazy for taking on the twins. For letting them drag me back into the mess I'd finally gotten out of. She… gave me an ultimatum. She told me to let them go to foster care or she'd leave." It was the first time he'd mentioned his ex in detail to London, and he felt her tense at his side.

"Any woman who'd say that wasn't worthy of them—or you."

"She had a background like mine. That… history. She

knew the potential for trouble. Addiction. She knows the statistics and odds are—"

"Cooper, stop. Don't borrow trouble or put something on the twins that may never happen. Have they had health issues? From the drugs their mother used beforehand?"

"Weight and growth-wise, they're small for their age, but so far everything checks out. I've been told that it could be years before cognitive and developmental issues appear, if they appear."

"Okay, then. *If* they appear, you'll deal with it. But right now, we claim victory over addiction and pray they never have any issues from that time in their lives."

London voiced the prayer without reservation or hesitation, and he stared at her in awe, both admiring her admission of faith and shocked at the same time by the trusting, carefree, and unreserved way she'd stated it, believed it, and pronounced it as a done deal. Thanks to friends' parents dragging him to church as a child, he knew the power of prayer, but he'd be lying if he said his life hadn't shaken that faith to the core.

But what good could come from the past? Dalton, his mother, Ashley's addiction. London was right. Maybe it was time to focus on the present and let the future play out however it was meant to. He wanted that prayer for the twins—and for himself. "Amen."

The barely audible whisper must've carried to her ears because London met his gaze. She nodded once, as if in satisfaction, and leaned back against his side.

They stared at the waves rolling in, the people—families—playing along the shore as though addiction and abuse and neglect weren't a thought, much less a reality. "I finished the project today."

London lifted her head, a smile on her beautiful, kissable lips.

"That's wonderful! We should celebrate."

There it was. An opening. His chance. Should he decide to follow through and claim that freedom and promise for himself. "We should," he said, thinking there was no time like the present to take that next step. "Maybe we could go out."

"Maybe," London said, lashes lowering over her beautiful eyes. "Another thank-you dinner?"

He waited until she made eye contact again before shaking his head. "No. This time we go because we want to see each other again. That is, if you're interested after everything you just learned about me."

Her expression softened, and a flush of color filled her cheeks that had nothing to do with the setting sun and everything to do with the chemistry firing between them. He wanted to kiss her, sensed she felt the same, but he didn't want to rush the moment.

No, he wanted to savor this. Her. Because this *was* different. London was different. And in that moment, he was very grateful for the painful lesson of his ex walking away, because he wouldn't be here otherwise.

"I'd like that very much."

"Tomorrow? Maybe we can rent a couple of Jet Skis or get a charter? You could show me around?"

"Actually," she said with a smile lifting the corners of her mouth, "that's totally doable because Carolina is already scheduled to work. I'm in."

Cooper stared down at her sweet face and couldn't help but think the same.

He was in… and free-falling fast.

Chapter 10

They stayed at the beach for quite a while, just sitting there watching the water and talking. He didn't say much more about Dalton. Truth be told, he wasn't sure what was left to say. He got the feeling London had a pretty good idea now that the blinders had come off. He hoped so anyway.

The shadows lengthened and darkness set in, but still they stayed. Cuddled and listened to the music being played at the pavilion as they sat on one of the many swings and gobbled up ice cream from the pier as their dinner to avoid having to be surrounded by people in one of the nearby restaurants.

Cooper walked London home and once again faced the challenge of leaving her at her door without a kiss. But considering they'd yet to have their first official date, he managed. Barely. But he reminded himself of his intent to savor the experience, all too aware that London was a woman worth the extra effort to romance.

Given the late hour, Cooper entered the house as quietly as possible and let Rocco into the yard for one last go, knowing the dog's escape launch had been moved to a better location. While he waited on Rocco to return, Cooper moved through the house, entering the kitchen upstairs since the fridge tended to be better stocked than the one in the apartment below. He opened the cabinet to grab a bowl, intent on some cereal to fill the void, when he saw a bottle of kids' liquid allergy medicine. Definitely not where that was supposed to be stored.

He shoved it into his pocket for safekeeping but then decided to forego the snack in order to check on the twins. Both were asleep, looking surprisingly peaceful. The sight tugged at his heartstrings and he moved closer to them. Both looked like Ash in some way. The way they'd tilt their heads or smile or laugh. It was easy to see Ashley every day just by watching them.

Cooper sat on the edge of Bella's bed and pondered London's statement about the future. He needed to play a more active role in the twins' routines. Be the dad he and Ashley had never had. Bedtime stories and tuck-ins. All of the rituals he knew to be stabilizing and good for kids but hadn't had himself. Like London said, he couldn't allow the past to dictate the future.

Ever since London's prayer about the twins, he'd felt more at ease. Maybe it was from relief that he'd told her the worst and she hadn't run screaming, but now… he felt more at peace with whatever the future held.

His stomach growled and Cooper leaned over the bed to kiss Bella on the forehead, catching a hint of something on Bella's breath. Something… sweet but medicinal-smelling. He frowned, hoping the girl wasn't coming down with a cold. Michelle should've called him. Informed him if so.

He felt Bella's forehead and the girl didn't move. No fever. That was good. Maybe just the sniffles?

Cooper shifted between the twin beds to Harry's and

bent to kiss his forehead only to pause, sniffing. Both kids' breath held the same scent.

Both were sick?

Kid germs tended to travel fast but something didn't feel right. He straightened and left the room, moving to Michelle's doorway, and knocked softly. "Michelle?"

The door was ajar, a light on by the bed. The bathroom door was open. She wasn't there.

He turned, listened intently to try to hear her if she was in another part of the house. Nothing. Surely she hadn't left the kids here alone?

He kept his office door locked due to the sensitive information he sometimes worked with, so that left—

Gut taut, he tiptoed down the stairs, glad Rocco was still outside and unable to raise an alert. A tread cracked beneath his weight and he grimaced but kept going, moving quickly past the door to the garage and the elevator door next to his apartment.

He opened the door to his private room with a silent twist of the knob. The TV screen flickered, on but silent.

It took a moment for his gaze to adjust to the dim interior, but he spotted Michelle asleep on his bed. Shock and anger filled him, but he had the presence of mind to grab his phone from his back pocket and hit the voice recorder app he used for work at times. Phone recording, he cleared his throat and flipped on the lights. "What are you doing?"

Michelle gasped as she awoke, the book she held tucked to her chest falling to the floor. The couple on the cover was barely dressed, and the title splashed across the bottom reading something along the lines of being *hot for nanny*.

"I-I didn't mean to fall asleep."

"Obviously, considering you're in my bed."

Michelle smoothed a hand over her hair, all remnants

of sleep gone as she stared up at him. She blinked at him, her expression changing.

"I was just— I mean…" She inhaled and shrugged, the wide neckline of the T-shirt falling off her shoulder and down her arm in response. "Why don't you join me?"

"Not going to happen." Now that the lights were on… "Is that my shirt?"

Her lips parted before she gave him a coy look.

"I spilled my drink on my pajamas and… I didn't think you'd mind."

"I do."

"Well, then I'll take it off."

She shifted onto her knees, hands reaching for the hem, and Cooper held up his hand. "Leave it. Are the twins sick?"

"No, why?"

"Because I found the bottle and they both smell like medicine. You gave them some?"

A guarded expression flickered across her face.

"Just a little. To help them sleep. It's perfectly safe. It's a little nanny secret," she said, shrugging like it was no big deal.

His hands fisted at his sides, and even though he knew the recorder was on, he fought to control his temper. The digital file wasn't admissible in court, but it could keep someone like Michelle from taking advantage of an otherwise innocent situation. "You're fired."

"What? Why?"

"You're seriously asking why? You *drugged* them."

"It's safe!"

"They're not sick."

"It's just to make them sleepy. It's not like they weren't on more in utero."

Michelle's eyes widened when he took a menacing step

toward her before stopping himself. "Come on. You're packing. Now."

"But—"

"You'd rather I call the police?" Odds were the police wouldn't take him seriously, and even if they did, he doubted Michelle would own up to it under oath. Things like that tended to happen in court, with people conveniently forgetting things they'd done wrong.

"Cooper, I was just trying to *help* you. You keep leaving the house because of the noise. You aren't getting your work done. I did it so you'd stay."

"There is no excuse for doing what you did."

"It's harmless," she said, sliding off the bed to her feet. "Like I said, all the nannies do it at some point."

He jerked his head toward the door, and she rolled her eyes and swiped the book she'd dropped from the floor. She gave him a wide berth as she walked past him.

Cooper followed her up the stairs, glad she didn't force him to get on the small elevator with her. In such close confines, he wasn't sure he could control his anger.

He trailed her to her room and watched as she yanked a suitcase from her closet. Her expression changed, darkened as a sneer twisted her lips and her beautiful face transformed into something ugly. Why hadn't he seen that before? Had he been so blinded by desperation for a nanny that he'd ignored signs he should've picked up on?

"You're going to regret firing me. Let's see how you do with those brats." She grabbed clothes and flung them into the suitcase before yanking on a pair of sweatpants. "I can't believe I *liked* you and wanted to hook up."

He bit back a comment and let the digital recorder roll, knowing his attorney would be proud of his forethought under the circumstances. Once she had a suitcase and large duffle packed, Michelle grabbed her purse and computer and stood glaring at him.

"Aren't you going to help me?"

He narrowed his gaze on her, pulled out his phone, and booked her an Uber to a nearby motel. "Your driver will be here in three minutes. Let's not keep him waiting."

Cooper kept the recording app running just in case, pocketed his phone, and moved into the room to pick up her luggage. "Take the elevator." He wasn't taking any chances and he didn't want her pretending to take a spill down the stairs and try to say he'd shoved her. If she was willing to drug kids, who knew what she was capable of?

Once Michelle was safely on the elevator, he closed the door and said he'd meet her at the bottom. No way was he riding down with her. Minutes later he dropped her bags outside the house just as the driver pulled in. "I'll pay you for this week but that's it."

Michelle glared at him and then told him off, and all Cooper could think of was that he hoped she hadn't used that kind of language around the kids. "Michelle?"

"*What?*"

"Be sure to put me down as a reference."

As the car pulled away with Michelle inside, Cooper turned to face the house with the twins sleeping inside, dread, panic and no small amount of fear stealing the breath from his lungs.

Now what?

Chapter 11

Saturdays were always busy days at the coffee shop whether in season or out. London worked the morning, but as noon approached and slipped right by, she started getting antsy due to the lack of communication from Cooper. They'd had some really good conversation, had opened up about emotionally weighty things. So… where was he?

Finally her phone buzzed and his name appeared, but when she unlocked the screen, it was to find him apologizing.

"Oh, I don't like that look. What's wrong?" Carolina asked. "It's something bad, isn't it?"

"He's canceling."

"What? Why?"

"Fired nanny last night," she said, reading the text. "Long story. Can't go on our date. I'm sorry."

"Oh, that doesn't sound good. I wonder what happened."

London worried her lower lip between her teeth and set the phone down to untie her apron.

95

"Are you going over there?"

"Wouldn't you? I don't think he's… kid-ready."

Carolina laughed at the statement. "Yeah, well, nothing like jumping in with both feet. Maybe you should let him handle things for a while. Just to let him get a feel for it."

"Trust me, if he's been on his own all morning with two toddlers, he's got a feel for it, wouldn't you say?"

"In man-world, yeah, that's probably true." Carolina grinned. "But you rushing over there just proves that you've got it bad."

"Stop it."

"Well, you do."

"Cooper is… a wonderful man. He's extremely smart, capable, fun. But I get the feeling he's at a loss when it comes to the twins."

"So go already. I've got this."

"You're sure you'll be okay here? It's been really busy today."

"Seriously? You doubt my coffee-serving expertise after how many years?"

"Right." Carolina was a whirlwind of energy, and if she did get backed up on orders a time or two, it wouldn't be for long. Besides, this was one of a few rare days London had pre-planned to enjoy before Cooper had even asked her out so… "Call Ireland or Mama or even Frankie if you need a hand."

"I'll be fine. Just go."

"Okay, yeah, I'm gone. Oh, wait!" London quickly grabbed a couple of sandwiches from those her mother had Carolina bring with her as well as quickly made two basic grilled cheeses and headed for the door.

She'd drive to Cooper's just in case she needed a vehicle later. Moments later, she pulled up to the only blue house on the street. It was nice. Really nice, actually. Big, like most of the newer homes here tended to be.

A familiar bark sounded from inside as she made her way up the steps to the second-floor entry. Cooper had mentioned having the best view from his office on the third floor and how he'd taken the room by the garage both for privacy and security's sake, so she figured the twins tended to rule the second floor on a normal day.

The door swung open right as she tackled the top step, and she saw Cooper on the other side of a screen door.

"London…? What are you doing here?"

She held up a bag of sandwiches and managed a smile despite her nervousness. "I thought you might not have eaten lunch under the circumstances. And… maybe you could use a hand?"

Cooper leaned heavily against the doorframe and stared at her, looking every bit like a man in over his head and drowning. His shirt bore multiple stains, there was a smudge of something highly suspicious on his cheek, and she was pretty sure when he got up that morning he hadn't put on swim trunks with a polo shirt, which meant whatever he'd worn before had been trashed by something, probably whatever had stained his shirt so badly.

"Are you sure you want to be here?"

Now that London knew about his ex's ultimatum, she knew what Cooper was asking, and it wasn't as casual as he tried to make it sound. "Yeah. I am. That is, if you want me here. I can leave the sandwiches and go if you'd rather." That last statement was a little harder to verbalize but she managed it. She didn't want to push, because if she'd learned anything about him during their conversations, it was that Cooper was a man who had to think things through. Plan. Formulate. It's probably what made him so good at what he did for a living, but it spilled over into his everyday life as well.

He stretched out a broad hand and pushed the screen door open for her. "Welcome to chaos."

Chaos was a mild descriptive for what she saw inside. Toys were strewn everywhere, the television blared, sippy cups and dirty dishes were piled high in and around the sink. All of this in a little over six hours or so? "You've been… busy."

"They won't eat. I've tried everything. I made eggs. Waffles. Toast."

London spied the results of Cooper's cooking and struggled to keep a smile from forming. That was some well-burnt food.

She turned when one of the twins came blazing through the room with a toy in his hand. "Harry?" The child stopped and stared up at her with wide eyes. "Hi, I'm London."

The little boy blinked but didn't say anything. Movement caught her attention, and she spotted a little girl sitting in the corner, playing with a doll. "And you must be Bella. Are you guys hungry? I brought food."

Both of them eyed the bag. "Do you like sandwiches? Maybe some grilled cheese, or a meatball sandwich?"

"You don't sell those at your coffee shop," Cooper murmured, the words close by her ear as he'd walked up behind her to get a look for himself.

"Mama sent them over this morning. Trust me, I don't normally share her meatball sandwiches, but for you, I'm making an exception."

"Thank God."

She laughed and pulled one of the specialty sandwiches from the bag and the fragrant smell filled the air. Cooper moved even closer, enveloping her in a near hug as he plucked the wrapped goody from her hand, and Harry and Bella hurried to climb onto the barstools, nostrils twitching.

Oh, yeah. Food was definitely the way to the heart.

Even little ones.

A LITTLE WHILE LATER, Cooper entered the living room and stared at London in awe. In the last hour, she'd played with the kids pretty much nonstop, giving him time and privacy to contact a childcare agency and set up interviews. He wasn't cutting corners this time and was unwilling to accept anyone's friend of a friend. He wanted a legitimate professional, and he'd go through the trying process of getting the right one no matter what it took.

The twins flanked London where she sat on the couch wearing one of Bella's tiaras, and all three of them watched a cartoon. Cooper started to join them but paused to grab his phone and snag a quick photo.

"Are you finished with the phone calls? There's a children's festival going on. I thought maybe we could go get some fresh air and exercise."

Cooper wasn't sure how London knew he was there since he technically stood behind them, but he made his way over to where they sat and perched on the edge of the nearby recliner, focusing on getting another picture rather than the terror instilled by her words.

He'd never gone anywhere with them. Not on his own. The thought of doing so twisted his gut. What if he *lost* one of them? They played in the yard every day, and Michelle had taken them places, but he had never actually... "Uh..."

"Hey, it's a beautiful day and I have coverage at the coffee shop. This way, we can still have our... date."

He met London's gaze. She called taking two very rambunctious twins to a festival a date? Keeping them corralled here in the house or fenced yard was way different than in public with other kids around and chaos thrown in. But London's expression... She actually wanted to do this?

"Cooper?"

London extracted herself from the twins and stood, tilting her tiara-ed head toward the kitchen. Bracing himself for the embarrassment to come, Cooper followed.

"Did you have trouble finding an agency?"

"What? No, I... They're scheduling interviews beginning Monday and sending a temp with thirty years' experience to watch the kids starting tomorrow. She'll be here before they wake up."

"Okay. But what about today? You plan to keep them cooped up in the house until the nanny gets here tomorrow?"

He ran his hand over his head. "We could... play in the yard."

Her gaze narrowed on him. "We just got back from there. You were on the phone."

"Oh."

"Cooper, it's a simple little festival. No big deal."

He inhaled and exhaled, grimacing. "It is. I've never actually... gone anywhere with them."

London's eyebrow lifted. She looked shocked for a moment before the expression shifted to one of understanding. Maybe even sadness? She squared her shoulders and settled her hands on her hips.

"Well, it's past time then, don't you think? And just so you know, I have years of kid experience what with babysitting and my nephew, so you're in good hands. Two of them, two of us? Those are pretty good odds," she said in a conspirator's whisper. "And it'll break the ice of you taking them in public without being completely on your own. So, what do you say?"

He glanced to where the twins sat on the couch, then back to London, looking insanely sexy in her blinged-out crown. "You're sure about this?"

"Why wouldn't I be? Ah," she said, tucking her palms into the rear pockets of her shorts. "That thing your ex said? Did?"

He nodded, hating that he had yet to be able to move beyond it bashing him upside the head whenever things like this came up.

London stepped closer. So close she had to tilt her head back on her neck to look up at him. He saw every fleck of emerald in her eyes, every freckle and the bit of glitter in her eye shadow.

She placed her hand on his chest and distracted him from his thoughts when her forefinger drew a slow, sexy circle on his pec.

"*You* are going to tell me more about this ex of yours," she stated firmly. "And why you fired your nanny in the middle of the night. But right now?" She tapped the costume tiara and tilted her head to a cocky angle. "Queen London calls the shots and I say we're going to a festival."

He chuckled at her declaration, her bravado, and dropped a quick kiss on her forehead, unable to help himself. "Well, Queen London, your wish is my command."

Chapter 12

Several hours later, Cooper's confidence had grown and he held a new appreciation for the woman at his side. Any time London sensed doubt or hesitation in him, she gently prodded him with a suggestion or two of acceptable choices. She steered them toward face painting and balloon animals, the petting zoo section that consisted of a duck, mini-goat, and horse. Away from the crowds that made him so nervous, because his first instinct was to look for an exit strategy should something go wrong.

Now he watched as London wiped Bella's mouth with a wipe, and instead of always fighting the act like Bella did when he tried to do it, the girl paid no mind to London. "Are you sure you don't want to give up the life of a successful business owner to become a nanny?"

London's laughter drew the attention of several nearby fathers, and Cooper felt a prickle of jealousy. He was really beginning to sense that she was a one-in-a-million girl and he'd be stupid to let such a woman walk away, much less push her away.

"And miss waking up at four a.m. every morning?"

"I'm sure there would be times they'd happily accommodate you. Me, too," he said in a teasing tone. He hoped it wasn't too soon to flirt on a more personal level when they still, technically, hadn't had their official first date. The entire day had been spent laughing and teasing, holding hands, touching and shoulder bumping in G-rated PDAs. The tension between them ratcheted up with every heated glance.

"Excuse me?"

He held up his hands as though proclaiming his innocence. "After the way you gobbled down the ice cream we got last night, I thought you'd be game for four-a.m. ice cream runs."

"Hmm. Did you share those late-night runs with the nanny?"

"Not a one. I promise. The offer is specifically"—he lowered his voice—"for you."

"Why, I do declare you flatter me, Mr. Bale."

He smiled at her overly dramatic southern drawl. "I mean it. You're great with them, London, but I can't wait until we get them home so we can spend some time relaxing together."

"You know, you're good with them, too," she said, shooting him an encouraging glance. "They test you but they respond well to your authority. That's no small thing given all they've been through."

No, it wasn't. He'd noticed that as well. Had they always been so well-behaved? He couldn't really say since today was the first time he'd spent any length of quality time with them, but they hadn't acted out or fought like they did at home with Michelle watching over them. Maybe because they were having fun and too distracted to focus so much on each other?

"I have to go potty," Bella said in her little-girl voice.

Cooper froze in the act of latching down one of the stuffed animals he'd purchased for his niece. "Can you hold it?"

"Noooo, I have to go *now*."

Panic seized him and he glanced around the park. Due to the event, there were several policemen talking to parents and event coordinators, but Cooper couldn't help but feel like a creeper at the thought of taking a little girl that wasn't his kid into the bathroom, niece or not.

"I'll take her. Relax," London said, placing her hand on Cooper's arm. "You like you're about to jump off a cliff."

"It doesn't seem appropriate since I'm not her—"

"You *are*," London stated, cutting him off before he could finish the statement.

He stared into Bella's dark brown eyes and realized she was listening and London had protected the little girl from his words. He nodded at London and inhaled, squatting down in front of the stroller to unbuckle his niece.

"You go with London, sweetheart. Harry and I will wait here, okay?"

Bella nodded and took London's outstretched hand. Cooper watched as they hurried away, and in the act of waiting for them, reality set in. Maybe for the first time. He was the parent of two almost-four-year-olds, and that meant doing things like taking them to the bathroom. Situations like this would come up again and he had to be prepared. But what would he do if he was alone? Send Bella into the ladies' room unaccompanied? Take both of them into the men's room? How did people do this? While he handled one kid, how did he keep an eye on the other?

What happened to his problems being what he wanted to do when he wasn't working? His next vacation?

He glanced at Harry and found the boy's head leaning

to one side against the stroller wall, eyes closed. Just like that. No need for drugs when exhaustion kicked in. "We'll figure it out, eh, bud?" Somehow.

After a long wait in the mugginess of the day, London and Bella emerged from the rest area, and Cooper watched every step. Heads turned as London walked by, and he believed it had more to do with the utterly beautiful, happy appearance she made rather than being known as the owner of a local business. London was breathtaking, natural. Maternal.

He added that quality to those he required in a nanny and hoped the agency was prepared to send him their best candidates.

London settled Bella into her stroller, and once she was strapped in, he fell into step beside London as she pushed Bella toward home.

"Cooper, this thing with Dally—"

"It's not a thing," he said, cutting her off because, after a fairly good day, the last thing he wanted to discuss was his drunk of an old man.

"No, I get that it's more serious but… I'd like to know more. That's all I'm saying."

Cooper turned the corner, and as he pushed Harry's stroller along the sidewalk, his mind traveled back to another time. Another place with carnival games and kids and parents. Dalton showing up drunk as a skunk, making lewd comments to the moms, and eventually getting beaten up by a couple of fed-up dads. "He's no good, London. Leave it at that."

"I know he's an alcoholic. But he's in AA."

A mutter left him that made him glad Harry—and now Bella—had both fallen asleep. "Like I said, maybe he's sober for now, but it won't stick. Never does. It's up to me to give these two a good life, and the worst thing I could do is let Dalton ruin their childhood the way he ruined ours."

"Even if Dally's changed?"

"No one changes that much." Silence followed his statement, but he caught the expression that flashed across her face. "You don't believe me?"

"It's not that. It's just something my parents always said. That it takes a village to raise kids and these two... they've lost so much. Their mother, grandmother. Biological father. If there's even a chance of their grandfather being involved—"

"There's not." A village. The bathroom incident with Bella had proven London's comment true about needing more people—trustworthy people—in his life for the kids' sakes, but for him that meant hiring a village. Nannies, teachers. Finding them a... mother?

It was too soon in their friendship to know whether or not London had potential in that area, but she'd done well today. Really well. She hadn't seemed to mind the twins' noise and messes. Truthfully London had handled them better than he had. Still, that wasn't hard for anyone to do considering his lack of parental skills at this stage, though he vowed to get better at the whole single-dad thing.

The rest of the walk was made in silence, and he wondered if London was the type of woman to pout or accept and regroup for battle later? Only time would tell, but her response would reveal a lot about her, and he was curious to find out more.

They made it back to the house, and Cooper opened the door and led the way to the elevator inside. He used the stairs almost exclusively, but one of the selling points of the large house was the small elevator for just such occasions as strollers, coolers, and sleeping toddlers. "London, I'm sorry. About having to cancel our plans," he clarified so she'd know he wasn't apologizing for his beliefs about Dalton. "In case you haven't figured it out, Dalton isn't a subject I like to discuss. There's no reason to when he's just not a part of my life anymore."

"You've written him off completely."

London leaned against the wall as the elevator began to move, looking saddened by the thought.

"He did it to himself. Look, London, I've already told you that my childhood was the polar opposite of yours in every way, but it taught me who I never want to be."

"I understand."

"Do you?"

"I do. It's… good that you know your boundaries. I respect that."

"Even if you think Dalton has changed?"

"Today was a fun day," she said, not answering his question. "I'm glad you accepted the outing challenge."

He moved closer to her, until they stood face-to-face. London looked up at him, all bright green eyes and full lips.

Another challenge? *Was* she the woman for him? "Are you?"

"Am I what?"

This time he didn't answer the question. He lowered his head but paused just short of her mouth. When she didn't pull away, he brushed his lips across hers, lingering over the contact and deepening the kiss when she released a soft sigh and slid her arms around his neck.

The elevator stopped on the second floor with a small lurch, and London gasped, smiling against his mouth.

"We, um, can't get out until you open the door."

Cooper ended the kiss long enough to glance down and found both kids still fast asleep. He settled his hands on the metal bar level with her hips and nudged her nose with his. "What door?"

Her hands tightened on his neck, and she held his gaze with a boldness he found insanely sexy. She tugged him low and he kissed her again, taking his time, reveling in every hitch of her breath, determined he wouldn't stop until they both forgot to breathe…

Chapter 13

"Hellllo? What's up with Pensive Penny?"

Later that same evening, London lifted her head from her knees but didn't take her gaze off of the rolling waves in front of where she and Frankie sat on a towel. "If you're talking about me…"

"You know I am," Frankie said, nudging her elbow into London's side. "You sure this sister summons isn't about you?"

London met her twin's gaze and nodded. "Positive."

"Fine. Then if you don't want to share with everyone when they arrive, get talking. What's got your brain wheels cranking so loud I can't hear the waves?"

London dug her toes deeper into the sand and tried to find the words to describe the unease in the pit of her stomach.

She and Cooper had packed the kids up and taken them to the festival in the park. They'd gotten their faces painted, oohed and ahhed over a puppet show, and played and run and jumped until their little legs had started to drag and they'd willingly climbed back into their strollers for the push back home. "I went out with Cooper today—and the twins."

"I see. How'd that go?"

"It was fun. Actually, it was a lot of fun."

"So what's the problem?"

"It… was also the saddest thing I've ever seen." She believed Cooper when he'd made the flirtatious comment being only for her about the four-a.m. ice cream fun. Maybe she was being naive about believing him, but she did.

Cooper had informed her of the nanny's antics throughout the day, all the while watching over the children like a hyper-nervous helicopter dad. During the course of the afternoon, Cooper had a tendency to hover, ask London her opinion of this or that, and work to keep a conversation going when it lagged. London could see where certain younger women might find Cooper's efforts and new-dad-knowledge-gathering attentiveness flattering, whereas he only saw it for what it was—information gathering to know how to be the dad he wanted to be.

"Oh, boy. Why?"

She explained to Frankie about how he'd fired the nanny, the state of the house when she'd arrived, and how he'd never taken the kids out on his own, along with the visible panic on his face when Bella announced her need to go to the bathroom.

"The guy is still getting used to things. It's not like he's had them from birth."

"I know but… there's more. I thought we were in a really good place, you know? The day went well. So, I tried to talk to Cooper about Dally."

"Oh, boy."

"Yeah. Cooper totally shut me out."

"You had to figure that would be the reaction, though,

didn't you? You know how weird families can be. You've said before how much you see just working in the coffee shop."

"I know. And from the little I've gathered, Cooper has reason to fear Dally being around."

"But?"

"But… it's Dally. And if he *has* changed and *is* sober, Cooper needs Dally around, needs him to be the father he wasn't when Cooper was growing up. Not to mention, those kids need a grandparent."

"Londy, I hate to burst your happy-little-reunion bubble, but kids need love and security, not toxicity. I get that you're concerned, but maybe you should focus on Cooper and let Cooper handle his relationship with his dad. Yeah? That way you don't get stuck in the middle of something you shouldn't be in. I mean, you weren't there and didn't live it, so maybe Cooper isn't all wrong."

"I know. I know," she repeated when Frankie shot her a disbelieving look. "It's just… Cooper seems so alone. He lost Dally because of his drinking, lost his sister and mom to death, and told me his ex left him because he chose to keep the twins rather than putting them in foster care."

"Wow. But if that's the case, he's better off without her. And so are you if you're interested in him," Frankie added with a pointed stare.

"It's just… sad. He's raising these two beautiful children with no family to help, and Cooper is so tied up in what happened in the past that he can't see the future and what it could be if… he could forgive them."

"Not all families are like ours. But it's better Cooper doesn't have help if it's toxic or has the potential to be."

But… it was Dally. And short of Cooper forgiving Dally, their family would never be healed.

She inhaled the salt air and tried to quiet her mind.

Maybe she'd put Cooper on the spot with her questions earlier, but she felt like they'd made it to the stage where the surface had been scratched and it was time to dig deeper. Especially if she planned to stick around.

"There's Caro."

Carolina approached them from the direction of the pier. When Carolina made it near the dream catcher mailbox, where London and Frankie waited, she dropped a towel to the sand before lowering herself. "What's up?"

"You tell us."

"Wasn't me. The number was new, so I thought one of you had gotten a new phone."

"Not me."

"Same."

"Ireland, maybe," Frankie asked.

"Holland is out of town again," Carolina supplied. "I'll bet it's her. Maybe something happened to her phone. What were you talking about when I walked up? You got quiet awfully fast."

"Nothing."

"Uh-huh. I work the entire day so you can spend it with Cooper and the twins, and you say nothing? Liar."

Carolina looped her arms around her knees and sent London a disbelieving stare.

"I'll fill you in later," she said to soothe Carolina's complaint. "I see Ireland. That's weird. She's coming from the opposite direction she usually does."

All of them turned to watch, and sure enough Ireland was coming from the south instead of the pier, where they usually made their way to the sand.

When Ireland joined them, she beamed with happiness.

"You're glowing," Carolina stated.

"I can't help it. Has Holland called yet?"

"No. So, did you call for this meeting or her? Who has the new number?"

"No new number for me," Ireland murmured. "But I was going to call a meeting so the timing worked out."

"Oh? What's going on?" London asked, more than ready for a distraction from her thoughts.

"And why were you coming from that way? Did you take a walk on the beach?" Frankie asked with a wave of her hand. "You should've told us so we could go with. I need some PT."

Ireland dropped to her knees atop Carolina's towel.

"I came from… my wedding present from Dominic."

London's mind focused on two words. "*Wedding* present?"

Ireland met her gaze, and before London could ask more questions, her phone rang with the strange number.

"Definitely Holland," Carolina said.

"Considering we're all here but her, it's pretty much a given," Frankie said with a teasing grin.

London slid the bar to answer the call and Holland's face filled the air. "Hey. New phone?"

A low groan filled the air. "Don't ask. Or better yet, do. Right, Ireland?"

Everyone looked at Ireland and found her smiling— and glowing, still.

"Okay, someone needs to fill us in," London demanded. "What's going on?"

Ireland sank her teeth into her lower lip before holding up her left hand.

"Uh, hello, we know you're engaged. You don't have to rub it in," Carolina said.

"Wait, are you wearing two— You *eloped*?" London gasped. "You actually did it?"

Holland laughed over the speaker as Ireland grinned and nodded.

The four of them shrieked, hugging, laughing, and scolding Ireland at the same time.

"I can't believe you got married without us," Carolina said, voicing their upset.

"Well, not all of you. Don't be mad but… Holland was there. We flew to St. Lucia since she was there for work. Holland was my maid of honor."

"I was just as surprised when they showed up as you are now. Trust me. I had no idea until it happened."

"We didn't want to wait any longer. If Dominic and I have learned anything, it's that life is too short," Ireland said, no doubt referencing the tragedy of Dominic's first wife, even though her death had brought them together.

"Are you pregnant?" Frankie asked.

"No! And you are *sworn* to secrecy," Ireland said. "If Mama finds out…"

"Oh my— Mom is going to *kill* you," London said, her gaze shifting from sister to sister until it landed on Ireland again.

"Which is why *we're* not going to *tell* her. This is a sister-hood secret. Pinkie promise."

"So what now?" Carolina said as they held out their pinkies to promise as asked. "We just pretend we don't know? For real? How long?"

"Until the wedding. Guys, I know it's a lot to ask, but I had to tell you. I couldn't hold it in. And I knew you'd be upset that Holland was there, but if we kept the secret *all the way* until the wedding, you'd really hate us."

"Got that right."

"So? We told you. Now promise," Ireland demanded.

"Promise," they said in unison, linking fingers just like

they had after sharing childhood secrets that never went beyond the five of them.

"So the engagement party is still on?" London asked.

"Yes."

"And the wedding?"

"Yes."

"You expect us not to slip up and tell Mom in *how* many months?"

"I believe in you. You can do it."

London finally remembered what Ireland had said walking up the beach. "And the wedding present from Dominic?"

Ireland grinned and London couldn't remember a time when she'd ever seen Ireland look happier. "We bought a house. Down that way. Oh, it's so beautiful."

"Wow. You're just full of news tonight," Frankie said.

"See why I couldn't wait? It needs some work, but we're hoping to have it ready to move into immediately after the wedding."

"You eloped, bought a house… Are you *sure* you're not pregnant?" Carolina asked.

Chapter 14

Sunday evening Cooper looked up at the sound of London calling his name and saw her leaning out of her second-story window above the coffee shop. The weather had been spectacular today, humid but breezy. All of the windows on London's second-story apartment were open, and the curtains billowed about her like white angel wings. "Hi, yourself."

She looked beautiful as always, her long hair loose and wavy around her shoulders and face.

"I'm almost ready. I'll be right down."

"No rush." He was curious about her home. Was she the type for clutter or a neat freak? Did she prefer more modern furnishings or antiques? "I'll be here."

Cooper took a seat in one of the colorful plastic Adirondack-style chairs lining the business and sidewalk and enjoyed the beautiful beach day. Birds chirped in the trees nearby; pelicans flew overhead toward the pier. Down the street, an older man walked alone, heading in Cooper's direction.

Cooper settled himself and took a deep, relaxing breath.

Tomorrow he'd start the next project on his list as well as enter day two of nanny interviews. Today's had gone well, though he hadn't been completely satisfied with any of the twelve applicants the agency had sent. He also didn't like having the interviews at the house, but he hadn't wanted to leave the twins with a total stranger, agency vetted or not. So his office sitting room had gotten a quick clean-up and eleven women and one man had put the small elevator to use.

"Evening. Nice night," the man said as he made it to talking distance.

"That it is," Cooper murmured.

The man carried a disposable coffee cup and pointed to one of the chairs by a table. "Mind if I join you?"

Cooper thought the request a little odd since it was obvious he hadn't purchased the coffee from London's closed shop, but waved a hand in agreement. "Help yourself."

The man sat and sipped his coffee.

"Haven't seen you around before."

"I'm new to the island but a resident."

"You got a family?"

Once again, Cooper braced himself for the small-town curiosity that came with living in a fishbowl. "Yeah."

"Good. Nice place for a family. How many kids?"

Cooper hesitated, not really wanting to give a stranger his life story even though he knew the nosiness was more than likely a conversation maker and nothing else.

"I thought I heard voices," London said as she stepped outside. "Dad, what are you doing here?"

Dad? Cooper looked at the man and could see amusement lighting his eyes when he spotted Cooper's surprise.

"Can't a man come visit his little girl?"

Cooper and London's father both stood at her exit

from the building, and London kissed her father on his cheek. "Not when it's to spy for Mama because she heard I was going out."

"I was walking back from seeing Samuel home after practice and saw your gentleman caller. Thought I'd get a bead on him. You understand, right, Cooper?"

Cooper laughed while London groaned. "That I do. Nice to meet you, sir. I'm Cooper Bale."

"Andrew Cohen."

"Dad, do me a favor and tell Mama Ireland's picked a date for the engagement party. I'll text her details but it's the weekend after Labor Day. Don't forget."

"I'll tell her. So, where are you two headed?"

London shook her head in warning at Cooper, and he remembered her comment about her family potentially showing up to grill him. "It's a surprise."

"I see. Well, you go have fun. Don't be out too late," Andy said to London. "Four—"

"A.M. comes early," London said with a nod. "I know. Believe me."

"Nice to meet you, sir," Cooper said to London's father. "London, are you ready?"

London quickly locked the door and then kissed her father. "Bye, Dad."

"Drive safe," her father ordered. "That's precious cargo you're taking with you."

"Yes, sir."

Cooper held out his hand and welcomed the small firmness of hers, looking both ways before leading her across the road to where he'd parked his black Rubicon.

"We have similar tastes."

"Oh?"

London pointed a finger, and he spotted a new-model

turquoise Jeep parked in a gravel drive beside the building. "Apparently we do. Nice color."

"My favorite."

He tucked that bit of information back for future reference, just in case, and opened the door for her to climb in.

The drive down Dow and then River Road took them to the restaurant. He'd made reservations. London had intrigued him enough that he didn't want anything to go wrong for this first official date with no kids in tow.

"Oh, I love this place."

He smiled at her words and pulled in to park. "I'm glad."

The restaurant bustled with noise and activity, and since they were a few minutes early, they took advantage of the offer to wait on the patio. The fire pits were empty due to the heat, but Cooper spotted two empty chairs away from the ant trail of people walking the river walk. "Over there?"

"Perfect."

They claimed the spot and a waitress quickly appeared to take their drink order. "Would you like to eat outside or are you waiting on a table?"

"Can we? Eat out here? It's not bad in the shade."

London looked so happy at the thought that he told the waitress to cancel their reservation for inside.

The breeze off the river kept them from getting too hot as the sun sank lower and pinkened the sky.

The waitress returned with their drink order in record time and he lifted his glass. "What should we toast?"

"Hmm…" She thought for a moment before saying, "To puppy love."

He smiled at the mention of Rocco and Rosie and how Rocco's disappearance had brought them here. "To puppy love… and new friends."

They clinked their glasses together and sipped, and Cooper had a hard time taking his gaze off of her. With her hair loose around her shoulders in organized curls and the shine of gloss on her lips, London drew him in a way no one had in years. Not even the former girlfriend he'd considered proposing to one day.

That thought sobered him. He'd never believed in the saying that everything happened for a reason, but if things happened as they were supposed to happen… well, he wouldn't be sitting here now, would he? Wouldn't have seen the difference in the two women.

"Tell me about today. The interviews. Any luck?"

"They were good but… I'm not convinced I've found the right person yet. And I was wondering if you'd help me with my search."

"Oh?"

"Yeah. The nanny did well with the twins today, which is why I felt comfortable leaving them for a little while tonight. So, I thought I'd have the agency send the interviews to the coffee shop. You seem to have that drink order thing you do down to a science, so I thought tomorrow you could keep an eye on the candidates as they come in and tell me what you think. If any of them stand out."

Her head tilted to one side and a smile pulled at the corners of her mouth. "While I am pretty good at it, basing their abilities as a nanny on their coffee order may not be the best way of going about hiring someone."

"It has to be better than the last time I tried it."

"True. However, I'd rather you focus more on their references than my skills."

"If you insist," he said, smiling at her. "But you'll still give me an opinion? Let me know if you notice something I might not?"

"Sure. Oh, and before I forget, I spoke with Carolina,

and she offered to pitch in if you need it. She's quite the free spirit and would probably drive you crazy at times, but she wouldn't drug them, lose them, or do anything else to otherwise endanger them. You could do worse as a fill-in until you find someone."

"I'll keep her in mind, but I plan to vet several professionals to have on call for backups."

"Backups for your backup?"

"I don't want to find myself in this situation again," he said with a nod.

London grasped her drink and took a long sip, her gaze holding his.

"It's going to be okay, you know. You were great with them yesterday, and while I understand your hesitation and worry that you're not ready to take them both on fully, you're a good dad, Cooper."

Her words sucker-punched him in an unexpected way. Stole the breath right out of his lungs. But that encouragement, that bit of praise went a long way in bolstering the doubts he had about... everything. Especially the next fourteen years or so.

"You know, the Fourth of July will be here before you know it and then Halloween. While you're planning ahead, maybe you should start looking for costumes."

"Uh, no. Besides, I don't want them overdoing it on sugar."

"Really? You're going to be *that* parent?"

"Ah, now the truth comes out. You want the twins' candy."

"Hey, I'll own it. My sisters and I used to meet and raid Samuel's treat bag after he went to bed. That was when he was younger, obviously, because now the little twerp counts his candy pieces so we can't eat any."

"You steal candy from babies," he murmured, giving

her a look of horror. "I *knew* there was something wrong with you."

"Hey, being an adult has a few perks and that's one of them. A girl's gotta get her chocolate fix somewhere, and it tastes so much better when it's contraband. That's all I'm saying. Besides, it's a crime if you don't take the twins out on Halloween and use that cuteness to your advantage."

"Does that mean you'll go with us if I take them? So you can teach us newbies how it's done?" There. For the first time, he mentioned the future. Him, her. Them. Plans that meant sticking around, at least for a while. Seeing where things might lead.

Was she up for it?

Was he?

"Mmm. Challenge accepted," she murmured as she lifted her glass once more. "Here's to... stealing candy from babies."

Chapter 15

Ah, the would-he-wouldn't-he question, London mused later that evening as she strolled along the river walk hand in hand with Cooper after dinner.

Would he kiss her again? When?

Their make-out session in his home elevator had gone on for quite a while, until one of the twins stirred and interrupted them. And ever since, she'd been on pins and needles wondering when it would happen again. Cooper seemed to be an affectionate guy overall. He'd held her hand as they walked to the restaurant and touched her often and left fire behind as a result. Chemistry-wise they had no issues. At least not as far as she was concerned.

And the mention of going trick-or-treating with him and the twins… Oh, she'd thought her heart would jump out of her chest. Scared though he was about the twins and her—their?—relationship or friendship or whatever this thing was between them, he was looking forward to the future. Thinking about it—them—together. And she liked that. She liked that a lot.

The sun sank lower in the sky and filled the horizon

with soft, cotton-candy-like color. Sunsets here were amazing, from fiery reds and oranges to the softer pinks and blues of tonight.

Cooper paused in a little viewing area along the walkway, and she noted they'd left the majority of the crowd closer to the restaurant and at the dock on the river.

They stood in the shadows of the trees hanging over the river walk, the breeze strong enough to lift her hair from her shoulders. She wrapped her arms around her front and hugged, because even though it was humid, the air held the slightest bit of dampness that left her chilled. "It's so beautiful here," she murmured, watching a pelican skim the top of the river as he headed south in the direction of Carolina Cove. "Sometimes I wonder what it would be like to live up north where it snows, or in the Carolina mountains, but then I look around and… it's our very own little paradise."

Cooper's hands settled on her shoulders briefly before smoothing down her arms.

"Are you cold?"

"No, not really. I'm fine."

He stepped closer and gently tugged her back so that she leaned against his chest, and he wrapped his arms around her from behind.

"Better?"

Mmmm. "Much," she murmured in response to his question. Why did it feel so good to be held by him? It wasn't like she hadn't dated other men, hadn't been held. But there was… something. Some thread or connection with Cooper. Well, at least it felt like it, but as she well knew, feelings could deceive, and chemistry, as lovely as it was, could fade. It happened far too often with couples who seemed to be perfect for one another.

They stood there and watched the sun sink lower until

it disappeared from view entirely. Once it was gone and the last of the rays were fading fast, she took a breath and turned.

One of Cooper's arms remained around her, holding her close, but he shifted his hand slowly from her back to her shoulder to her neck as she moved, and once she faced him, he used his hold to tilt her chin higher. She met his gaze, held it despite the intensity that made her want to close her eyes or look away, in case she was alone in this—whatever this was.

Cooper lowered his head, and a sigh escaped her as he lightly touched her lips with his. The kiss began sweetly. Just a gentle little swipe of his mouth across hers. But she relished the feel of him holding her, sliding his hand along her jaw, beneath her hair to cradle her head, as he pressed a little harder and deepened the kiss to something more.

He tasted like sweet tea, smelled like mint and sandalwood and spice. Felt like heat and hardness and a headiness that left her clinging to him for balance.

Cooper drew her closer, and she reveled in the warmth of him at her front and the cool breeze along her back. Her heart raced in her chest, a mixture of nerves and excitement and pleasure, her senses bombarded by him.

Someone laughed in their general vicinity, and she suppressed a groan of complaint when Cooper's chest tensed beneath her fingertips. He ended the intensity of the kiss but lingered over the contact.

It took her a moment to muster the will to open her eyes. She wanted to stay in that darkened cocoon. Stay in that place of comfort and synergy and amazingness where nothing else existed except for the two of them.

It took her a moment longer to realize Cooper's entire body had turned to stone and it had nothing to do with them kissing. "Cooper?"

She turned to see what held Cooper's attention and spotted the couple standing several feet away. "Uh… Dally? G-good evening. My, don't you spiff up nice." She'd never seen Dally dressed up. The older man wore khakis and a nice polo instead of the fishing wear she was used to seeing him in. For the first time, she noticed Dally and Cooper shared the same height and lankiness in build.

"Hey there, London. Cooper. It's good to see you. This is Marilyn. It's our anniversary."

"It's a pleasure to meet you, Marilyn," London said, hyperaware of Cooper's silence. "Dally's told me what a wonderful woman you are. Happy anniversary."

"Thank you."

"Cooper, your stepmother's a—"

"She's not my anything."

"Cooper." London gaped up at Cooper, shocked he'd be so rude to someone who, like her, had nothing to do with the past between him and his father.

The two men stared at one another, and Dally's expression broke London's heart because the man looked so sorrowfully at his son, earnestness etched in every deep line of his pale face.

"We're leaving," Cooper said, turning his back on the couple.

London dug in her heels, torn between propriety and — "Cooper, *wait*," she urged softly.

Cooper released her hand and kept walking.

"I just want to see my grandkids," Dally called after Cooper. "Spend time with them. With *you*. Please, son."

London watched as Cooper kept walking, his long strides eating up the boardwalk at a record pace as he moved from the shadows to the lights lining the pathway. She turned to look at Dally and Marilyn and found the older woman holding Dally steady as he quietly sobbed. "Dally, I'm sorry. I am."

"I know, sweetheart."

"I-I should go. It was nice meeting you, Marilyn. I'm *sorry*."

Dally gripped the cane he held tighter, leaned heavily against Marilyn as she led him toward a nearby bench.

London hesitated once more to make sure Marilyn was able to get the heartbroken man settled but then hurried after Cooper, jogging to catch up with him. "Cooper." He didn't slow down. "Cooper, will you please slow down?"

Her request must have sunk in because he slowed his pace—a bit. She hurried to close the distance in case he took off again. The moment she could, she grabbed hold of his arm.

"I want to get out of here."

"I know. But did you see him? *Really* look at him? Something is *wrong* with him, Cooper."

"There is a lot wrong with him, London."

"Stop? Please?"

Cooper finally paused in the breakneck pace, his chest rising and falling heavily as he was the one who'd practically run the entire way to that point and not her.

"Cooper, I get that he was a bad person at one point. A bad father. But that's not the Dally I know, and one look at him tells me he's seriously ill. Surely you saw that back there? Because I can testify to the fact that in a month's time he's... he's gone downhill fast."

"Like I said before, fifty years of drinking will do that to a man."

"*Cooper*. You're angry. I get it."

"Do you?"

"Yes! I do. But that's the past. Will you ever let it go? If the answer's yes, then why not now?"

"You're on his side."

"I'm pulling for *both* of you. Why can't you understand that?" She placed her hand on his arm and squeezed it tight. "Cooper, if he was the man you've described, I wouldn't push it. I wouldn't," she said when his gaze narrowed doubtfully. "I-I just don't want you to regret it if something bad happens. Tonight… that's the worst I've ever seen him since the first day he came to the coffee shop."

"And when was that?"

"What?

He stared down at her in six feet plus of handsome anger.

"When was that? When did he show? How long has he been coming there?"

"Uh." She had to stop and focus long enough to recall. "It was in… May. Yeah, it was May. I remember because it was when…"

"Rocco showed up," he said, growling the words. "When I brought my mom here before she passed away."

"But… how would he have known you were here?"

"Mom. She probably told him. Despite everything he'd done to her, she kept in contact." He shook his head. "Unbelievable. She was as codependent as they come and still considered him the love of her life." The sound that emerged from him lacked all hint of humor. "What a life it was."

"It sounds as though… they may have made peace with each other."

He didn't respond.

"Cooper, I can't begin to comprehend what it was like growing up with a drunk for a father. You didn't deserve that. No kid does. But you're an adult now and you have to let the past go. You're breaking the cycle with the twins. You've uprooted and changed your entire life for them, but if you truly want to be the father they need, it means letting yourself heal and putting it—who Dally was—behind you."

"Don't. I can't stand here and listen to you defend him. You don't *know* what he did to me. To Mom and Ashley. If you had any idea… f you *knew the hell…*"

His voice carried the horror of it, and her heart shattered for him. For the little boy he used to be who'd needed his dad not to hurt or yell or… "Don't do it for him, Cooper. Do it for yourself. For the twins. Forgiveness isn't just about your father. It's you being able to let it go and living the life you should've had from the very beginning." She slid her arms around his waist and cuddled close, breathing in the scent of spice and man.

London felt his lips brush her forehead, press against the top of her head as he swallowed her in an iron-hard hug. She listened to his heart beat beneath her ear and measured the words that formed. "Cooper, you can run from something or you can run to something. If you run from, it's out of fear and pain, but if you run to?" She lifted her head from his chest so she could meet his gaze, hold it. "It's because of love a-and hope. Because you want something better for the future. For you and your children."

Cooper wouldn't meet her gaze. He stared at her but didn't see her, and she knew he was lost in the memories tormenting his mind.

"That man will do nothing but hurt those kids if I let him."

The arms locked around her dropped to his sides and she felt bereft. "So don't let him. You're their guardian. You have full control. No one will argue that right. But if Dally is as bad as he looks… Cooper, he's their only grandparent."

"So? They meet him and then what? I have no reason to believe anything has changed."

"But if he's sober—"

"That would be a miracle, London. And I lost my ability to believe in them long ago."

She wrapped her arms around his middle and hugged him close once again and rested her forehead on his chest even though Cooper didn't return the embrace.

"I want to go home. I don't want to leave the temporary nanny for long, fully trained and experienced or not."

Cooper extracted himself but snagged her hand in his for the walk back to his Jeep. "Cooper… the kids would never have to be alone with him. Never have to go anywhere with him."

"Not going to happen."

"Even if he *has* changed?"

Cooper released her hand and opened her door but didn't wait for her to get in. He stalked around the front of the vehicle to his side and jabbed the key in the ignition the moment he settled in his seat.

"He hasn't."

"Cooper—"

"Drop it, London. Okay? All of the what-ifs don't apply here. The man *destroyed* my mother and my sister and he very nearly destroyed me. Why would I give him the chance to do it again? It's up to me to protect Ashley's kids, and I owe her that since I wasn't there when she needed me. There are no compromises here."

"There could be. Cooper, don't you see? We have no control over choices people make in life. It's on them, not the ones who love them. You are not responsible for Ashley's choices, and like it or not, neither is Dally."

"That's where you're wrong. Had he been a better man —a better father—Ashley would be here today."

"You don't know that. Dally could've been sober, the best father ever, and she still might have made the same choices."

"I won't invite him back into our lives just so he can wreck them again. London"—Cooper stopped and shook his head, fairly vibrating with anger—"Dalton's made a decent impression on you, but that's not the real him. Now, either you support me in this or we need to end things between us, because I'm not going to spend another moment of our time together fighting about him."

"HE *SAID* THAT TO YOU?" Frankie demanded an hour later after London texted her sister the private, twin version of 911 and Frankie had appeared on her doorstep minutes later with Tank in tow.

"Yeah." London curled up on one end of her old couch, loving that everything in her home smelled like richly brewed coffee and chocolate. When it came to scents, those were a natural de-stressor for her, and living above the coffeehouse in the old building made her apartment a cocoon of comforting goodness. "But I'm telling you there's something really wrong with Dally. He had a cane and was obviously really, really weak. Whatever is wrong, it's serious. I'm worried about him."

"Cooper isn't."

London watched as Frankie joined her on the couch and motioned for Tank to hop up between them. Tank was officially a retired bomb-sniffing K-9, but he had the personality of a comfort dog with his laid-back demeanor, which was probably why Frankie was letting him on the furniture. "What am I going to do? Cooper and I haven't known each other long but it's been… There's something there. Something real and good that I'd love to explore."

"Are you sure it's not his hot body?"

London gripped her cup of tea in both hands and made a face at her sister. "You sound like Carolina."

"Well, from what I've heard, he is hot. Too bad he's so screwed up."

"He's not screwed up. He's…"

Frankie waited for London to finish the sentence but she didn't. Couldn't. Because they both knew it was a lie. Cooper had deep-seated family issues due to his childhood, and London wasn't sure how to help him cope or even if she could. "You should've seen him yesterday. He was terrified of taking the twins out because he'd never done it before, but he was a natural. Kind and attentive, firm when he needed to be. He could have easily turned out to be a drunk or an addict like his sister, but instead it's like he's *over*corrected and gone the extreme opposite."

"Which confirms the fact that if you push too hard…"

"I risk pushing him away for good," she said with a sad nod. "He's already pulling away from me. I could feel it tonight when he brought me back here. He dropped me off and didn't kiss me. He just… left."

"Do you think he'll come to the coffee shop tomorrow for the interviews as planned?"

"I hope so. He has quite a few scheduled. Maybe in between them we can… talk."

"Talking got you in trouble. Maybe just laying one on him would be a better plan of attack."

Frankie's comment drew a smile from London, and she shifted her attention to the German shepherd lying on the couch between them. "What do you think, Tank? Should I just kiss him?"

Tank's ears twisted and shifted in response to his name

and her touch on his hindquarters, but when she began stroking his thick fur, he lowered his head back onto Frankie's thigh.

"Okay, so, tomorrow you'll get your chance to smooth things over. Let him cool off tonight and get some distance. Maybe things will be better come morning, and he'll see you're only trying to help. He can't stay mad at you, Londy. No one can."

"Mmm. If you say so."

"I do."

Frankie lifted a hand and smothered a yawn.

"I'm keeping you up. Go home. Get some sleep."

Frankie waved away the suggestion. "I'm good."

"You know, maybe you'd sleep better if you let yourself relax when you start yawning and such."

"Sleep is overrated."

Uh-huh. Frankie wouldn't say much about the nightmares she suffered from, but London knew they kept her from ever getting a whole night's sleep. "You wanna stay here? We can share the bed or you can unfold the couch."

Frankie tilted her head to the side and lifted an eyebrow high.

"Stop worrying about me."

"You're exhausted. You're *always* exhausted. Have you ever thought about getting some counseling for the PTSD?"

Frankie sighed and flashed London a glare.

"This is why we can't have sleepovers anymore," she said sternly, pushing herself up off of the couch.

"Frankie, you don't have to leave."

"I know. But maybe if I do, you'll realize you have enough to worry about without adding me to your list."

Frankie waited while London stood and then hugged her.

"I'm sorry," London said to her sister. "Apparently I can't keep my mouth shut tonight."

"Just go to sleep. It'll be better in the morning."

London watched them go and locked the door behind them.

Maybe Frankie's prediction would come true. Maybe Cooper just needed time to mull over what had happened. What she'd said to him, the condition they'd seen Dally in…

Or maybe the hours between now and then would allow Cooper to retreat even more.

Either way, it was a crap shoot. But for the second time that night, London had driven someone she cared for away, and she didn't like how it felt.

Chapter 16

Cooper hurried down the sidewalk, figuring he'd arrive about the same time as his first interview candidate.

He'd tossed and turned most of the night, London's words replaying in his head along with the memory of her hurt expression when he'd told her support him or else.

That'll get you boyfriend points.

But was that what he was? A boyfriend? Or just a friend? Someone London felt obligated to help because of reasons only she understood?

Now really wasn't the time to be trying to figure out such things, but when he thought about London and life… she seemed to fit like a puzzle piece that had been missing.

Unlike Dalton.

Dally.

Cooper shook his head at the nickname. Why had Dalton used it with London? How had that come about?

Only way to know is to ask him.

Yeah, not happening.

When Cooper had fallen asleep, he'd dreamed a mixture of old Dalton and new. Room-destroying rages from when he was a kid when Cooper was forced to grab Ashley and make a run for it to hide themselves in a closet or jump out the window to hide on the roof. They'd stay hidden or gone until Dalton passed out and wait for the morning, when he'd wake up and pretend nothing had happened.

But the new Dalton, old, beaten down, hobbling along on a cane and looking like death… What was up with that? And how had Dalton managed to score a woman who, by the looks of her, seemed normal? Well dressed, pulled together, and considerate if her hold on Dalton and the worried expression she wore were any indication.

His *stepmother* had seemed… loving. Kind. Normal.

Then again, the only other woman he'd ever seen Dalton with was his mother, who'd stopped taking care of herself early on due to the emotional, verbal, and random physical abuse Dalton had bombarded her with.

He arrived at the coffee shop and paused for a split second with his hand on the door, inhaling in an attempt to brace himself to see London. He knew he ought to apologize for his behavior last night, but the anger he'd felt at her taking Dalton's side still ate at him.

"Mr. Bale? Good morning," a woman said the moment he walked across the threshold.

He looked over to find a very plain woman who looked to be in her early thirties. She appeared much older, however, due to the old-fashioned skirt that fell to her ankles and the long-sleeved shirt she wore despite the muggy heat outside. "Uh, you must be my nine o'clock."

"Yes, sir. Prudence Symmes. I was early. The early bird gets the worm, right?"

"Uh, sure. Have a seat."

"Where would you like to sit?"

"Anywhere." She blinked at him, wide-eyed, but didn't

move. Finally he turned toward a table by the windows and pulled out a chair. She quickly followed and sat down opposite him. "Would you like coffee?"

As though conjured by his words, London appeared, looking every bit as sleepy-eyed and tired as he felt. Apparently they'd both had a restless night. "Good morning."

"Hi." She set a large mug of black brew on the table in front of him.

"He didn't order that. I was here the whole time and he didn't order that," Prudence stated emphatically.

"I know but—"

"Take it away. He doesn't want someone else's order."

"Uh, Prudence, I'm a regular here. London knows my order."

"Oh. Oh, of course. I didn't realize."

"Mmm," London said, her expression strained. "What can I get you… Prudence, was it?"

London stared at the other woman rather than make eye contact with him.

"I'd like a latte heated to no less than 140 degrees, with organic soy. Not fake organic. True, certified organic. Oh, in this."

London's expression probably matched his own when Prudence pulled a saran-wrapped mug from her purse.

"Please leave the wrapping on the handle until you bring it to the table, then unwrap it and take it with you."

"Okay, then." London accepted the mug from the woman who set it on the table rather than actually hand it to London and turned, catching his gaze briefly before looking away.

"Excuse me for a moment, would you, Prudence?" Cooper got up and followed London to the counter. "Hey."

"Hey, yourself."

"London…"

"Germaphobe or control freak."

"I'm sorry?"

"You asked me to help you by giving you an assessment of their orders."

"Right. I did."

"Well, this one is a toss-up. What's she going to do with the twins? Wrap them in plastic or berate them for not following orders?"

"Good question. London, I'd like to apologize for last night."

London leaned against the counter, and he fell deep into the sea of green looking back at him.

"We disagreed. People disagree all the time, then they talk and make up. It's fine."

"Is it?"

She tilted her head to the left and shrugged. "I hope so. Does it mean you'll at least *think* about talking to Dally?"

"It means I'm sorry I took my upset with him out on you. That's all." The history between him and Dalton was just that—between them. London need not be involved.

London shifted to go back to making Prudence's order. "I can handle that. We're not there yet, are we?"

"Not just yet."

She nodded. "Well, you know where I stand on forgiving Dally."

"I do."

She nodded again and took a deep breath.

"So, uh, do you want me to mess with Prudence by taking off the wrapper just so you'll see how she'll respond?"

Cooper couldn't hold back the chuckle that emerged at the thought. "I triple dog dare you to do it."

London shared a grin with Cooper before she gleefully ripped off the plastic wrap. Cooper turned to follow her back across the room when his phone buzzed with a Wilmington-area number. The temporary nanny?

London set the naked mug on the table in front of Prudence.

"Here you go."

"Excuse me. What did you do?"

"I brought you an organic soy latte heated to 140 degrees."

His phone buzzed again and he slid his thumb across the screen to take the call, listening in on the conversation at the table with complete interest. "Bale."

"You took off the wrapper. I told you *not* to remove the wrapper until you brought it here to the table. Can't you follow simple instructions?"

"My apologies." London grabbed the towel hanging from her apron string and wiped off the handle. "Is that better?"

"No, it's not better! Who knows what you've done with that rag you just used, and now it's spread all over my handle. How do you run a business?"

"Cooper," a woman asked in his ear. "Is this Cooper Bale?"

"It is. Who is this?"

Prudence stood, holding her hands in front of her like the coffee mug was going to jump out and bite her with all of its microscopic germs.

"I'll make you another."

"I don't have another cup. Why couldn't you simply follow instructions? Leave the wrapper on the handle. Is it that hard to understand?"

"I'll get you some plastic wrap," London said in a reasonable tone.

Cooper caught London by the arm as she turned to walk past him and shook his head. "It's fine."

"This is Marilyn Hewes-Bale, your— Dalton's wife. Please don't hang up. Dalton's in the hospital. In ICU. It's bad, Cooper. He's been sick for some time. He wants to see you. You and the twins, in case he doesn't make it. Please just… consider it. I'm begging you."

"Cooper? Are you all right? Who is that? Something with the twins?"

"Hello?" Prudence said. "I'm not finished talking to you."

Cooper held his hand over the end of his phone. "The interview is over. Thank you for your time."

"But… we didn't even get to talk because of her mistake." To London, Prudence said, "Do you see what you've done?"

London ignored the woman and placed her hand on his arm, concern etched in her features. *Who is it?* she mouthed.

"What hospital is he in?"

London's expression changed to one of understanding as Marilyn gave him the name and address.

"Cooper, please hurry," the woman said, voice choking on the words before she ended the call.

"What is it? What's wrong? Did something happen to one of the twins?"

He shook his head, tried and failed to rein in his racing thoughts.

Prudence gathered her purse and glared at London but left the contaminated mug on the table as she stalked out the door, muttering the entire way about following instructions.

"Cooper, you're scaring me."

"Dalton's in the hospital. He's asking to see me and the twins in case he doesn't make it." London's hand flew to cover her mouth at the news, and he saw the pity and empathy in her eyes. "Do you know how many times I wished that man dead? Now here it just might happen."

And the kicker was he wasn't sure how he felt about it. Because what if London was right? What if Dalton had changed? What if it had taken a lifetime for him to get his act together and now he had, but it was too late?

That would be Dalton's luck.

His, too.

"What are you going to do?"

He stared into her gaze, lost to the thoughts bombarding him. "I can't— I can't go…"

"Oh, Cooper."

"Not without you. I can't— London, will you come with me? Please?"

He'd surprised her with the request. She'd expected him to say he wasn't going, wasn't going to honor the request. He'd thought about it, for sure. Why should he go? Why should he do anything for Dalton?

But almost as quickly as that thought formed came another. That of London telling him to forgive Dalton, for his own sake if nothing else. Because the fact was, he didn't want the last impression of Dalton to be of the raging drunk who'd terrified him for so long.

"I-I will. Of course I will. I'll call Carolina while you go get the twins. Or close now and Carolina can open right back up," she said, appearing to think through the plan aloud. "It won't take her long to get here. She or Ireland or my mom can come. Whoever's free. None of that matters. Of course I'll come with you." She gripped his hands in hers and held them tight. "I'll be right beside you."

IT WAS TAKING TOO LONG. That was all Cooper could think as he drove through the midday bumper-to-bumper summer traffic. London had closed up and called Carolina on the walk-run to his house while Cooper had called the temp and told her to have the twins ready by the time they arrived.

Now, almost an hour later, he pulled into the hospital parking lot and swerved into an empty space. Bella began fussing in the backseat because, once they were stopped, she didn't like being strapped in.

They unbuckled car seats and grabbed the strollers so that London would have them should she need them while he and Dalton made their peace. Dealing with the kids was a process, and it wasn't a fast one, especially with Bella acting out.

Finally they hurried down the long corridor toward ICU, and with every step, Cooper prayed it wasn't too late. Whether it was because he wanted to have his say or simply say goodbye, he wasn't sure. He wasn't sure about much of anything at the moment.

"There's Marilyn," London said.

He looked around but then did a double take at the white-smocked woman moving toward them. It was her, though. Dalton had married a doctor?

"They just updated me. He's stable, for now," Marilyn said by way of greeting. "Thank you for coming. They don't normally allow children in ICU, but given the circumstances, they're making a very brief exception so long as I'm with them. No more than a minute or two, tops. Just for him to see them."

"What happened?"

London voiced the question and Cooper waited anxiously for the answer.

"The drinking," she said simply. "He's on the transplant list for a liver, but as of now, one isn't available."

"I'm... surprised he's allowed to be on the list at all."

London looked shocked by his statement but Marilyn simply nodded. "Transplants will be given to those sober six months or longer, and Dalton's been sober ever since Ashley's death."

"That was over three years ago. He's... never made it that long that I know of."

Marilyn nodded. "No, he hasn't. But losing his daughter changed him. He felt responsible and knew he had to be sober in order to be of any help. That's where we met, actually. In AA," she said, her gaze direct. "I've been sober twenty years, and while every day is a battle, as a physician I can tell most times when that switch has been flipped, and I knew, when your father shared at a meeting, he meant it when he said he was done."

Shock rolled through him. Suspicion. For all he knew, Marilyn was the same type of codependent woman as his mother. Except... she wasn't. He could tell. Marilyn was strong, confident. Everything his mother had never been.

"You should go in first," London said softly. "Talk to him. Then we can take the twins in."

Cooper nodded and followed Marilyn to Dalton's hospital room. He paused outside the door, wondering if he had what it took to step inside.

Chapter 17

After Cooper finally entered Dalton's room, Marilyn approached London and the twins.

"I should probably confess that Dalton didn't ask to see Cooper or the babies."

London gasped in surprise but just as quickly nodded, exchanging a wry smile with the older woman. "But you know he wants to."

"It's all he's ever wanted since I've known him." Marilyn lowered herself in front of Bella's stroller. "What's the matter, baby? Has she been pulling on her ear long?"

"Uh, I have no idea. I haven't seen her since Saturday but… come to think of it, I think I remember her doing it a few times then. Oh, no. Ear infection?" she asked, remembering the telltale sign from when her nephew would do the same.

"Could be. How about we take a walk and find out?"

London fell into step beside the woman who grabbed the handles of Bella's stroller and began slowly pushing it down the corridor. "Dally said it was your anniversary?"

"Yes. We've been married a year." Marilyn smiled at

London. "He asked me six weeks after we met but I made him wait."

London laughed. "I can see Dally doing that. He's a character."

"He can be. He is also the sweetest man I've ever known. Life humbled him in ways only a few can imagine and made him a better man because of it."

"I'm glad I didn't know the other version of Dally." London followed Marilyn, thinking of Cooper and wondering how he was holding up given the circumstances…

Chapter 18

Cooper entered the room, the noise of the machines masking the sound his footsteps might have made. Dalton lay in the bed with his eyes closed, an oxygen mask over his face. "Dalt— Dally," Cooper said softly, the word—the nickname—bringing a lump to his throat.

His father opened his eyes as though the weight of them was too heavy to bear. When he realized Cooper stood by the bed, Dalton's eyes widened, a weak smile breaking over his haggard face.

"You're really here? Not… dreaming?"

Cooper nodded. "Marilyn called and said— It's good you're on the transplant list. That you've stayed sober."

The awkwardness was there, though it was tempered by necessity. The saying that it was hard to kick a man when he was down was very true. All of the things he had to say suddenly didn't seem important because Dalton bore the weight of them already. They were etched in every line and shadow, echoed by every bleep of the machines.

"Too late now."

"Not yet. It can still happen."

"No. Meant too late… for you."

Cooper inhaled and knew this was the moment of reckoning. He had to decide between the man he could be and the man he wanted to be. The man he wanted the twins to have as a father. "It's not too late. London… She says we either run away from something or run to it. The first one is in fear but the other—"

His voice locked up and Cooper cleared his throat, but the words just wouldn't return.

"I got my miracle," Dalton said weakly, a smile hovering on the corners of his mouth. "You. Here."

Cooper took Dalton's hand in his and squeezed. After a long moment, he cleared his throat again. "I—we—brought the twins."

Dalton's eyes filled with tears and overflowed. He lifted a trembling hand and tried to rub the moisture away, but the mask got in the way and the move seemed to exhaust him given the quivering attempt.

Cooper grasped his father's hand in his and lowered it to the bed before snagging a nearby tissue box and pulling one from the cardboard. It took every ounce of control he had in him to calmly dab at his father's tears and not think of the times Dalton hadn't been there to do the same for Cooper.

"Son… forgive me. Please. I didn't know what I was doing. Stupid, stupid fool. I'm sorry. I'm so sorry."

Cooper paused, the wet tissue fisted in his hand and a lump in his own throat. The man he could be. Or the one he wanted to be. He had to choose and be able to live with the consequences of his choice. "If… If you're going to be allowed around the kids, you have to stay sober. No exceptions."

Dalton's tears increased and Cooper set out once more

to catch them. "But that also means you have to hang on until you can get that transplant."

Dalton nodded. Lifted his hand and grasped Cooper's wrist, squeezing it.

"The twins need you. London reminded me that they don't have a grandfather. And I never knew— Dalton, I never knew the sober you. But if you can hang on, I'd really like to meet that man."

Dally's face broke as a sob tore out of him, and Cooper leaned over the bed and hugged his father for the first time in over twenty years.

THIRTY MINUTES LATER, he and London were heading out of the hospital with the twins. Marilyn had prescribed some medication to help with Bella's inner ear infection, and now they prepared to make the drive home to get the twins settled with the nanny so they could return to the hospital for the evening visiting hours.

Cooper settled into the driver's seat once the kids and London were tucked inside, but other than turning the key to cool the interior, he didn't move.

"Are you okay?"

The twins had visited Dalton for a brief moment. The last—the only?— time they'd see their grandfather?

"Cooper—"

"I love you." He stretched out a hand and slid it beneath her thick braid, cradled her neck, and gently tugged her toward him. "I didn't expect— I thought it would be better to do this alone. To do life alone. Easier. Safer," he said, staring into her beautiful face while tilting his head back to indicate the twins. "But I don't want to."

"You don't have to."

"Are you sure? You want this mess? The craziness?" He paused. "Me?"

She shifted so that she could close the distance separating them and touched her lips to his mouth, her eyes open so he could see everything and know she meant it. "I'm sure. I want it all—especially if the crazy means you."

FIVE MONTHS LATER, London felt Cooper before she saw him. She closed her eyes and reveled in the sensation, and seconds later, his hands spanned her waist and his lips settled in the ticklish part of her neck.

"There you are."

"Mmm. I was sidetracked by the full moon," she said, enjoying the breeze off of the hotel's oceanfront patio. "All okay in there?"

"As far as I can tell. Your mother is happy at pulling off the wedding in such a short time span, Samuel is snitching cupcakes whenever anyone's back is turned, and Ireland and Dominic are beaming about the baby."

Surprised, she turned in his arms, twining hers around his neck. "You *know*?"

Cooper dropped a kiss atop her nose.

"Only because I spotted Dominic in the parking lot and caught him staring at an ultrasound photo."

Her laughter echoed off the side of the building. "Busted," she murmured. "At least Mama got her fancy wedding reception even though Ireland had to come clean about already being married due to the pregnancy that made being a June bride tricky. "Where are the twins?"

"Marilyn and Dalton went with Jenny to take them home to put to bed," he said, referring to the nanny hired not long after that fateful trip to the hospital. Cooper's list of qualifications had bordered on the ridiculous, but she had to admit he'd found a good one to fill in any gaps that her mother and father, Dalton and Marilyn couldn't handle.

Dalton had several near-death moments but managed to hang on until a transplant donor had been found in October. With the twins and Cooper as incentive, Dalton had made a miraculous recovery, determined to spend what time he had left being the best father and grandfather he could be to make up for his past.

"Have I told you how beautiful you look tonight?"

"Several times."

"Have I told you how much I love you?"

She grazed her fingers over the short stubble of hair on the side of his head, loving the feel of it. "You know I can't hear that often enough."

"Well… I love you, London Cohen."

He lowered his head and kissed her, lightly at first before deepening the caress until she clung to him and struggled to stay upright in her fancy bridesmaid's shoes.

"Sweetheart—"

"Mmm?"

"Marry me."

The whisper left her gasping. She opened her eyes and found him watching her, waiting.

Holding her gaze, Cooper lowered himself to one knee, and in the distance, she heard the sound of her mother's excited shriek.

London barely dared to breathe, not wanting anything to ruin this moment.

"What do you say?" He opened a small velvet box and pulled a breathtaking emerald and diamond ring from the folds. "Will you take me, the twins, and Rocco and Rosie, and whatever else may appear in your coffee shop one day, and love us forever?"

She held out her quivering hand for him to slide on the gorgeous ring. "I will, I *have*," she said, bending to kiss him, "from the very beginning."

CAN'T GET ENOUGH OF THE COHEN SISTERS? KEEP READING FOR A SHORT EXCERPT OF MAP OF DREAMS:

Fuming because Holland seemed to have some sort of sixth sense where Carolina was concerned, she stalked toward her car and tossed her purse inside the open window. The roar of an engine turned her attention to the driveway and she gasped at what she saw. "Seriously?"

It was the truck from the school. The *man* from the school. He'd followed her home!

Heart in her throat, she waited as he rolled the large truck to a stop. His windows were down and she yelled to be heard over the powerful engine. "What are you, some kind of stalker?" Her heart rate increased as panic set in. There were way too many weirdos in the world and people who took offense to the slightest thing. *Like stealing parking spaces.* She pointed to the street. "Leave. Right now. I'm sorry for cutting you off this morning, but that's no excuse for you to follow me."

"I'm—"

"*I'm* calling the cops and you'd better be gone before they get here."

He muttered something under his breath. "Put the phone away."

She pressed the phone's emergency button to call 911 so that he could see her do it.

"Are you crazy?"

She spotted a Carolina Cove police car driving down

the street toward the station located a few blocks away and waved both of her arms. "Hey! Hey! *Help!*"

The man released a mutter she couldn't hear over the engine and the blood pulsating past her ears. She rushed to where Officer Bobby Binet pulled into the driveway. Thankfully she knew all of the policemen due to working at the various businesses in town. "Bobby, thank goodness."

"What's going on?"

Officer Binet quickly got out and eyed her unwanted visitor, who cut the engine and exited his truck with a slam of the door.

"He followed me home because of road rage after I took his parking spot earlier. I told him to leave but he won't."

Bobby crossed his arms over his chest and looked way too casual for her taste. Shouldn't he have his hand on his gun or something? Push her behind him and tell the man to stand down?

"Hey, Silas."

"Bobby. Good to see you again."

She stared at the two men as they greeted each other, mouth gaping. "*What?* Bobby, *do* something!"

"She's got it all wrong, brother."

"I do not have it wrong! He got mad at me at the school and then followed me home."

"Silas? That true?"

"Not by a long shot."

"It is! There's no reason for him to show up here like some crazed perv."

"Crazed perv? Lady, for the love of— I didn't follow you home."

"You're standing here, aren't you?"

The man ran his hand over his head and down to his neck, muscles flexing as he squeezed.

"Silas," Bobby said, walking closer to where the other man stood, "what's going on?"

"I just told you," Carolina said, growing even more aggravated by Bobby's lack of concern and lackadaisical manner.

Silas held up a hand as though telling them to wait and walked back to his truck.

"Watch him, Bobby. He could be getting a gun."

"Calm down. Silas isn't doing anything of the— See?"

The man turned, holding a bunch of papers clipped together, and Carolina got an uneasy, sinking feeling in her stomach.

"I didn't follow her home. I came," the man said, waving the papers, "to get to work."

This couldn't be happening. Holland was going to kill her. The man so angry with her after her stunt at the school would have to stand in line behind her sister to take a whack at this particular mole. "W-work?"

The word emerged as a strangled squeak that sounded way too guilt-ridden for her tastes. Maybe it was the heat of the day but… she actually felt a little light-headed.

Was it possible to pass out from embarrassment? What were the odds?

Seriously.

Silas shoved his sunglasses up on his head and gave her a baleful glare. "This is 114 Seashell Lane, right?"

"Yeah, but—"

"You're Holland Cohen?"

"She's Holland's baby sister," Bobby explained. "Carolina Cohen. Carolina, this is Silas Fletcher. Didn't I hear something about you working for Jake now?"

"Yeah. Her sister hired McMurphy Construction to work on her house. I'm here," the man said, giving

Carolina yet another glare, "as Jake's foreman. The crew is scheduled to start today."

"Aw, now there you go. See, Carolina?" Bobby said. "Just a coincidence that y'all ran into each other this morning at the school. It's all good."

All good? This was *good*? She'd just made a total fool of herself in front of the man for the second time that day, called him a crazed perv... and Bobby thought it was good? "I didn't... I saw you pull in and I thought— You were *really* angry this morning," she said, sounding defensive to her own ears. "I mean, where's your sign?"

"What?"

Did he have to look at her like she was a complete airhead? *Did she have to* feel *like a complete airhead?* "On your truck. Shouldn't you have a sign? So people know who you are and don't think you're—"

"A crazed perv," Bobby said, chuckling as he shot Silas a broad grin.

"I-I was going to say *robbing them* but... yeah."

Silas looked at the offending truck in question and then back to her. "This is my personal vehicle. The company truck I usually drive is in the shop."

"Well, you should have a sign," she said irritably, like the stupid sign actually mattered more than her manners or lack thereof. But if he'd had a sign on the truck, she would've immediately known who he was when he pulled in. Better still, if she'd seen it at the school, she would've known not to cut him off, and this entire disaster wouldn't have happened. "I have to go. I-I'm late for work."

The abrupt announcement left both men staring at her like she'd grown two heads, but after the run-in at the school and now this, she'd be perfectly fine if a sinkhole opened up and swallowed her so she never had to see Silas

Fletcher again. Instead, she'd probably be seeing him every day for the next few weeks?

Unless he quits and then you won't see him because you'll be dead, murdered by an angry Holland who just wanted her repairs done. "I… apologize." She ignored Bobby's ongoing grin and wished the man wasn't wearing a badge—or a gun—so she could…

What? Make things worse? "The signed contract is on the counter along with the keys to the house. The door off of the patio room is open. Just… call Holland if you have questions. I should… I *really* have to go."

She hurried to her car, glad she'd tossed her purse inside and didn't have to go to the house and reappear while the men watched. She was mortified enough the way it was. Maybe if she left early enough in the mornings she wouldn't have to see Silas Fletcher?

But Holland had said all of the work would take at least eight weeks, weather permitting. But how could she avoid the man for that length of time when he was working at the house?

You wouldn't have to avoid anyone if you hadn't made such a scene.

Face flaming, she climbed into Pearl, hands trembling as she started the little Bug and shot down the driveway, squeezing between the giant truck and Bobby's cruiser with both men watching her every move.

She glared at Silas in her rearview mirror and, strange as it sounded, felt like they actually made eye contact despite the fact his gaze was once more hidden by his dark sunglasses.

He'd changed shirts, she noted. Was that why he was late? She'd bet the new blue shirt really brought out the color of his eyes now.

Carolina groaned, shook her head at her thoughts, and punched the gas.

CLICK THE LINK TO CONTINUE READING MAP OF DREAMS . HAPPY READING!

THE SEASIDE SISTERS SERIES:

THE LAST GOODBYE
LATTES AND LULLABYES
MAP OF DREAMS
WORTH THE RISK
LOST LOVE FOUND

Books Also Set in Carolina Cove

CAROLINA COVE SERIES:

- SEASCAPES AND VEGAS MISTAKES
- SEASHELLS AND WEDDING BELLS
- SEA GLASS AND SECOND CHANCES
- SEA BLUE AND LOVING YOU
- SEA VIEW AND SOMETHING NEW

MAKE ME A MATCH SERIES:

- ROMANCE RESET
- RULES OF ENGAGEMENT
- THE MATCHMAKER'S SECRET
- PERFECTLY MISMATCHED
- BY THE BOOK

THE SEASIDE SISTERS SERIES:

- THE LAST GOODBYE

- LATTES AND LULLABYES
- MAP OF DREAMS
- WORTH THE RISK
- LOST LOVE FOUND

Excerpt of Sea View and Something New

Isn't it funny, she mused, how failure opens one's eyes to true fear?

Sophia Shipley studied the outdoor patio and its well-dressed guests, careful to keep her turbulent thoughts masked behind a ready smile that showed none of the terror coursing through her body like electricity.

She'd left Carolina Cove, North Carolina, for college at eighteen and been on the fast track to success ever since. High school valedictorian, class president, lacrosse captain, cheer captain, and more scholarships than she could count. Her streak continued throughout college and again once she'd joined the workforce, but standing here now, in this moment, weighted with secrets, her spiral into the depths of failure had yet to slow. She'd thought leaving Raleigh in shame was her rock bottom, but now that she was here she realized it was just the start. Her heart raced in her chest, her grip on the champagne glass in her hand turning painful.

Tessa and Bruce Holloway danced, the newlyweds

beaming with love and happiness. Sophia's heart squeezed at the sight and loved the fact that, despite their divorce in the 1970s, the couple had found their way back to one another again. Tonight was all about them, as it rightly should be. Which is why she needed to focus on the happy couple and not on the stress making her pulse pound in her ears.

She took another sip of champagne and glanced around the gorgeously decorated patio. The wedding planner had outdone herself. Cheryl Dummit had offered up her gorgeously landscaped yard as the location for the reception, and it looked breathtaking with its soft twinkle lights, candles, and decor.

A gorgeous glittery-gold backdrop took up on side, the perfect spot for guests to perch on a lush cream velvet settee for photos. It was all just... wow. Sophia couldn't imagine pulling together all the little details for something like this, but then again, that's how Eliza Bellefonte-Hayes had earned her reputation as the best wedding planner in the area. Some even said the state and beyond.

"You seem pensive," a voice said from behind her. "Is everything all right, Sophia?"

Sophia turned and sucked in a silent gasp. Barbara Lancaster, business woman of the year too many years to count, stood nearby, a glass of champagne in her hand. "Barbara, hello. It's good to see you."

"You as well. I wondered if you'd...make it back for this event," the older woman said carefully.

Sophia felt the color drain from her face.

She knew. "Barbara, I'm not sure what you've heard but I can assure you, gossip is rarely accurate."

Barbara's gaze narrowed into a shrewd stare and she took a long sip from her glass, staring at Sophia over the rim the entire time. After a moment of silent contemplation and a swallow, Barbara spoke.

"So the rumors are false? You haven't… quit the finance business?"

Sophia battled the hot flush of mortification that threatened to turn her body into lava, and forced her lips into a semblance of a smile. "Well, I suppose they are true then. Yes, I've taken a step back from the industry."

"And your step back has nothing to do with Bernard Pitz?"

Sophia faltered, aware of the tightrope she walked. The non-disclosure agreement was quite specific in terms and one whiff of a breach could land her in jail. "Barbara, you of all people know how it is. The rat race is insane and… after watching my cousins and sister find their significant others, it occurred to me what kind of sacrifices I'd truly have to make and…I'm just no longer sure that's what I want."

Barbara's expression made it clear Sophia could talk until the sun came up but the woman knew the truth. And didn't buy an ounce of Sophia's version of it. "Look, Barbara, the financial community is relatively small and I can only imagine what you've heard but you've been a close family friend all of my life which is why I'm asking you to not say anything to anyone. My parents don't know the details of my resignation and I'd like to keep it that way."

"I understand. But I'll just say this. Thirty-two years ago I worked with Bernie on a project and he was a putz and lech even then—and I wasn't nearly as beautiful as you. I'm sorry it—whatever it was— happened. And that you had to take blame for it."

"Barbara…" Sophia's voice trailed off as she battled

the sharp sting of tears. Once again, she forced a smile in response to Barbara's implication.

She could do this. She would do this. Her career in finance might be over for reasons beyond her control but considering the circumstances, however unfair, she'd hold her head high. She chose to look at it as an opportunity to begin anew. To find her second passion and succeed with it. It was all a matter of setting her mind to it. "Tell me— How are you doing? Mama said you might go with the Babes on a Girls' cruise."

Barbara's expression made it clear the change in topic was noted but thankfully the older woman allowed it.

"Perhaps. I haven't decided yet. Will you be in the area long? Perhaps we could have lunch?"

A huff left Sophia's lungs before she could stop it. Literally no one in her family knew of her job loss or situation, yet Barbara had hit on everything Sophia had tried to avoid discussing the evening after her arrival. "I will be, actually. I signed a short-term lease today."

"Here? In Carolina Cove?"

"Yes. My family doesn't know yet," Sophia said, lowering her voice to give weight to the need for privacy. "So again, please, don't mention it?"

If Sophia hadn't known Barbara most of her life she wouldn't have trusted the other woman with the information but it was only a matter of time before she had to come clean with her parents. "It was spur of the moment and I'd like a few days or a week to myself before having to take on everyone's questions. Plus with all of the wedding preparations I didn't want my news to take any of the spotlight away from Tessa. I'm sure you understand."

"That's sweet of you, dear. Though I'm sure Tessa would understand your family's excitement that you're back in town. The Babes must be thrilled."

During the summers of '58 and '59, four of the prominent Carolina Cove neighbors and friends had given birth to baby girls.

The proud mamas had taken the five girls for daily strolls in their prams—and the locals had nicknamed the group the Boardwalk Babes—a name used to this day by the sixty-somethings.

"Though I do wonder how you think you're going to stay in the area under their noses for any length of time and not be discovered," Barbara said.

Sophia laughed and downed the last of her glass before exchanging it for another. "It may be a pipe dream but I'll take whatever time I can get."

"Rest assured your secrets are safe, my dear. It's been lovely talking to you and I do hope you'll be in touch regarding that lunch."

"Of course," Sophia said. "Maybe after I'm…settled." Barbara was sharp as a tack and maybe by then Sophia would have some business ideas to run by her and get her thoughts on.

"Yes, well, I'm going to go say my goodbyes. I have work to do before bed. Oh, I do envy you right now," the woman added. "I can't imagine having free time to sit and ponder life's possibilities."

Sophia forced a light laugh but it held no humor. She watched as Barbara walked away and took a fortifying sip.

Barbara had touched on every secret Sophia carried due to stupidly trusting the wrong individual. And even though she had no one to blame but herself, the thought of starting from scratch scared her to no end. What if she couldn't do it?

"Rumor has it you're out of the game," a deep male voice said. "Yet here you are schmoozing. Looks like the spoiled rich girl didn't learn her lesson."

THAT WAS AN EXCERPT FROM SEA VIEW AND SOMETHING NEW AVAILABLE FOR PRE-ORDER NOW!

SEA VIEW AND SOMETHING NEW

Also by Kay Lyons

MONTANA SECRETS SERIES:

- HEALING HER COWBOY
- IT HAD TO BE YOU
- HERS TO KEEP
- MILLION DOLLAR STANDOFF
- HIS CHRISTMAS WISH
- THEIR SECRET SON

THE SEASIDE SISTERS SERIES:

- THE LAST GOODBYE
- LATTES AND LULLABYES
- MAP OF DREAMS
- WORTH THE RISK
- LOST LOVE FOUND

TAMING THE TULANES SERIES:

- SMALL TOWN SCANDAL
- THEIR SECRET BARGAIN
- CROSSING THE LINE
- THE NANNY'S SECRET
- SOMEONE TO TRUST

THE STONE RIVER SERIES:

- WORTH THE WAIT
- NOT BY SIGHT

- THROUGH THE VALLEY
- LEAD ME NOT
- CHRISTMAS AT HOLLYWOOD
- THEIR CHRISTMAS MIRACLE
- SECOND CHANCES

SMALL TOWN SCANDALS SERIES:

- BRODY'S REDEMPTION
- FALLING FOR HER BOSS
- WITH THIS MAN

SECRET SANTA SERIES:

- SECRET SANTA
- SECRET SANTA II: A CHRISTMAS TO REMEMBER

MAKE ME A MATCH SERIES:

- ROMANCE RESET
- RULES OF ENGAGEMENT
- THE MATCHMAKER'S SECRET
- PERFECTLY MISMATCHED
- BY THE BOOK

CAROLINA COVE SERIES:

- SEASCAPES AND VEGAS MISTAKES
- SEASHELLS AND WEDDING BELLS
- SEA GLASS AND SECOND CHANCES
- SEA BLUE AND LOVING YOU
- SEA VIEW AND SOMETHING NEW

About the Author

Kay Lyons always wanted to be a writer, ever since the age of seven or eight when she copied the pictures out of a Charlie Brown book and rewrote the story because she didn't like the plot. Through the years her stories have changed but one characteristic stayed true— they were all romances. Each and every one of her manuscripts included a love story.

Published in 2005 with Harlequin Enterprises, Kay's first release was a national bestseller. Kay has also been a HOLT Medallion, Book Buyers Best and RITA Award nominee. Look for her most recent novels with Kindred Spirits Publishing.

For more information regarding her work, please visit Kay at the following:

www.kaylyonsauthor.com

@KayLyonsAuthor (Twitter)

Kay Lyons Author (Facebook)

Author_Kay_Lyons (Instagram)

Kay Lyons, Author (Pinterest)

SIGN UP FOR KAY'S NEWSLETTER AND RECEIVE UPDATES ON NEW RELEASES, CONTESTS, PRE-RELEASE BOOK INFORMATION, EXCLUSIVES AND MORE!

www.ingramcontent.com/pod-product-compliance
Lightning Source LLC
Chambersburg PA
CBHW011600190726
48287CB00010B/2980